To Be a Rose

To Be a Rose

E.B. Mason

ARPress
45 Dan Road Suite 5
Canton MA 02021
Hotline: 1(888) 821-0229
Fax: 1(508) 545-7580

Ordering Information:
Quantity sales. Special discounts are available on quantity purchases by corporations, associations, and others. For details, contact the publisher at the address above.

Printed in the United States of America.

ISBN-13:   Softcover   979-8-89389-434-9
                    eBook   979-8-89389-435-6
                    Hardback   979-8-89676-245-4

Library of Congress Control Number: 2024917387

For Anne
You were always there even when I was someplace else

United States Department of State
Bureau of Consular Affairs
Washington, DC 20520

This information is current as of today, Mon Jun 06
12:51:23 2005

AFGHANISTAN

November 15, 2004

"This Travel Warning provides updated information on the security situation in Afghanistan and on the upcoming Afghan presidential inauguration event. The security threat to all American citizens in Afghanistan remains critical. This Travel Warning supersedes the Travel Warning for Afghanistan issued July 30, 2004.

The Department of State strongly warns U.S. citizens against travel to Afghanistan. There is an ongoing threat to kidnap and assassinate U.S. citizens and non-Governmental (NGO) workers throughout the country. The ability of Afghan authorities to maintain order and ensure the security of citizens and visitors is limited. Remnants of the former Taliban regime and the terrorists operations continue. Travel in all areas of Afghanistan, including the capital Kabul, is unsafe due to military operations, landmines, banditry, armed rivalry among politician and tribal groups, and the possibility of terrorists attacks, including attacks using vehicular or other Improvised Explosive Devices (IED), and kidnapping. The security environment remains volatile and unpredictable.

Presidential elections occurred on October 9, 2004 with minimal disruptions. However, the potential for violence remains a real concern. In the wake of the elections, a suicide grenade attack killed an American citizen in downtown Kabul, and three U.N. International staff were kidnapped in late October 2004. Presidential inauguration events in early December may trigger additional violence.

There have been a number of attacks on international organizations, international aid workers, and foreign interests and nationals in the past year. The United Nations has resumed operations, which were temporarily suspended in the aftermath of these attacks. However, the UN continued to be the target of attacks throughout the country. 1 June 2004, a UN and NGO convoy was ambushed in Gardez, a UN demining team was ambushed with rocket propelled grenades (RPGS) in Loghar, and a United Nations High Commissioner for Refugees (UNHGR) convoy was ambushed with RPGS and small arms fire in Kandahar. Over the past year there have been multiple rocket attacks in Kabul and elsewhere in Afghanistan, including a rocket that landed in the International Security Assistance Forces (ISAF) compound near the Embassy in June 2004.

Family members of official Americans assigned to the U.S. Embassy in Kabul are not allowed to reside in Afghanistan. In addition, unofficial travel to Afghanistan by U.S. Government employees and their family members requires prior approval by the Department of State. From time to time, the U.S. Embassy places areas frequented by foreigners off limits to its personnel depending on current security conditions. Potential targets include key national or international government establishments, international organizations and other locations with expatriate personnel, and public areas popular with the expatriate community. Private U.S. citizens are strongly urged to heed these restrictions as well and may obtain the latest information by calling the U.S. Embassy in Kabul or consulting the embassy website. Terrorists' actions may include, but are not limited to, suicide operations, bombings, assassinations, carjacking, rocket attacks, assaults or kidnappings. Possible threats include conventional weapons such as explosive devices or non-conventional weapons including chemical or biological agents."

I had read that before I left the United States and was mentally prepared for it going in. What I was not prepared for was how I was going to leave.

Part One: The Beginning

Kabul, Afghanistan, August, 2005

"I can't breathe."

"Sorry, I didn't understand what you just said."

"I can't breathe. I can't complete a sentence . . . without taking a breath."

The Army Combat Medic picked up a stethoscope from his desk to examine my chest. I started to take off my shirt. He told me that wasn't necessary. At the time I thought, *How are you going to hear anything through a heavy canvas shirt and a cotton T-shirt?* There was an Army doctor, a Colonel in charge of the Aid Station, working in the background attending to other business.

"Any history of lung disease?"

"Yes, about eight years ago . . . when I lived in Italy . . . I was told it was a mild case of pneumonia. It was cured with a thirty-day regimen of pills . . . which normally only a horse . . . could swallow."

While he was examining me, I was thinking about how I got to Afghanistan.

I worked for a defense contractor that hired primarily retired Army and Air Force Lieutenant Colonels and Colonels to provide a host of outsourcing advice and hands on capability to the United States military. We had a contract with the U.S. Army to augment their effort to establish a proper Army of

Afghanistan. Our office was in Camp Eggers, named after an Army Special Forces Captain who was killed during the initial invasion of Kabul. I was hired as a Senior Logistics Expert to work with the Afghanistan Ministry of Defense as an advisor and mentor to two senior Afghan officers. I arrived in Afghanistan earlier that year and had settled into a daily routine. I had a feeling today was not going to be routine.

After listening to my chest, he told me to sit on the exam table and take off my shirt and dog tags. He stuck suction cup monitors to my chest and side. It was interesting to see the results. It was a portable EKG monitor used by the U.S. Army in battlefield medicine. When he received the printout revealing my condition, everything was flat line. Probably, the battery was dead or the device malfunctioned. He put a clip on my left hand middle finger that had a wire attached. I asked him what it was for. He explained it was to measure my oxygen saturation level: It was 61 percent. I found out later it's supposed to be about 98 percent. I asked him jokingly if this indicated I was dead. "No, but you will be if we don't get moving."

Certain words have associations with places you've been or things you have done. When I was a young Captain in the U.S. Air Force, I was assigned to a Fighter Squadron based in Germany. Our Squadron would deploy a month at a time to Zaragoza, Spain to train on the Spanish bombing ranges. Due to our flying schedule, as the maintenance officer, I had to be on the flight line by five o'clock in the morning. One morning, as the big Spanish sun was cooking up over the horizon creating beautiful brushes of yellows and oranges, there was Roberto's morning visit. He drove a mobile food van which the Airmen called the Roach Coach. Because his English was limited, he would pull up on the flight line and step out and sing what you would expect at an opera; "Rooooach Cooach!" He sold little Spanish pastries, coffee, juice, and fruit to the GIs at the break of dawn. I was in line behind one of my Airman who had ordered a coffee. When Roberto served it, it had an insect floating in it.

"Hey! There's a bug in this coffee!" Roberto calmly looked at the cup and said, "It no moving."

He pulled out a white plastic spoon to remove it. Due to the fluid dynamics, he couldn't catch it. The bug kept swirling around in perpetual motion. He poured it on the ground and made another cup. I don't know why, after the medic mentioned the word "moving" it cast my memory back to Spain. I guess it was a premonition of what was to come. *It no moving.* I was about to be the bug and encounter perpetual motion.

An Army field ambulance ride can be an interesting experience. I was helped onto an Army stretcher and loaded into the ambulance. We were going to Camp Phoenix where there was an ISAF field hospital, the first level of medical care for battle wounded manned by multi-national forces of the European Union. In addition to the driver, there were two U.S. combat medics in the back with me. Both had M-16 rifles, one sat by my side with his weapon balanced between his legs and the second sitting by an open hatch in the rear with the barrel of his M-16 pointed out the window. I knew the route through downtown Kabul and was aware of the hazards. Those two young medics were going to make sure nothing happened to me.

As we were moving through Kabul, the familiar smells of the fifth poorest country on Earth were present. There was a constant smell of smoke produced by street vendors who would burn anything they could find to fire their sidewalk grills which were usually made from fifty-gallon drums that were cut in half. They would cook lamb and chicken to sell as a snack for people who were out and about. The acrid smoke from the grills added to a continuous orange brown cloud over the city from automobile and truck emissions. There was no unleaded gas in the country. Additionally, there was the constant smell of some kind of organic material, I once had a conversation with an Army Occupational Medicine Doctor who told me that twenty percent of the particulates suspended in the air was the dust from dried fecal matter or the remains of dead animals or people.

I knew we were passing the walls of the American Embassy when the scent shifted from poverty and dust to the roses of Kabul. Even though there were no windows in the ambulance except the back hatch, I could identify where we were based on the lateral movements of the vehicle. I knew when we passed the Massoud Circle, past the lifeless-looking five-story apartment buildings built by the Soviet Union during their twenty-year occupation, many still with bullet holes, and then a straight line dash through dust to the outskirts of Kabul and onto Camp Phoenix.

Camp Phoenix, outside of Kabul, Afghanistan, August, 2005

The Field Hospital was an International Security Assistance Force facility. It was not a proper building, rather a tent city that looked like an Army M.A.S.H. unit. There were no hospital beds, just treatment tables. The concept of medical care was: If you were a member of the Coalition forces and were wounded or sick, you would be stabilized and evaluated for movement on to the next level of care. From there it would be to Baghram Air Base, a U.S. Air Force Hospital and if serious enough, MEDIVAC by an Air Force C-17 to the U.S. Army Hospital in Landstuhl, Germany.

When I arrived at Camp Phoenix, I was transferred from a stretcher to a treatment table. The tables were made from high tech foam about three inches thick sealed with clear plastic. They were wrapped in a crisp light green sheet. I was between two soldiers who had stepped on land mines left over from the Soviet occupation. A German was on my right and a Dutchman was on my left. Both had heavy bandages on their right feet and blood was weeping through the gauze. I was immediately administered oxygen through a clear plastic mask and evaluated by an Italian doctor. Two German nurses were present and the doctor told them that I was not to fall asleep. It was easy to understand because the two official languages of NATO are English and French.

"Nicht Schlafen!" the Nurse commanded. So much for the official languages of NATO. I suddenly understood this was going to be a long night.

Dance the night away. . . .

The two German nurses were exacting in obeying the medical orders, and in retrospect, I'm glad they were. They played "tag team," reminding me every five minutes, all night. This marathon reminder gave me a chance to remember the sights, sounds, and the smells of Afghanistan and my journey there. As I lay staring at the ceiling of the tent, I had twelve hours to think about it. A flight of ideas, memories, and those two nurses kept me awake. I laid on my back all night trying to remember how I got there, considering I had never been hospitalized a day in my life. I had spent twenty-two years as an officer in the U.S. Air Force, primarily as a Logistics and Engineering Officer. I had been heavily involved in International Logistics spending a great deal of time working in the Balkans, North Africa, Turkey, and the Middle East. My work in Afghanistan was a natural continuation to what I had been doing for the bulk of my adult life.

"Nicht Schlafen!"

Breathing is getting hard . . . keep going.

"Did you ever notice that ocean salt water cures hemorrhoids?" He lifted his drink, took a big slurp and wiped his mouth on the back of his hand.

"No, Ralph. I haven't given it much thought. I have noticed that ocean water is salty but never thought about it curing hemorrhoids because I don't have them."

"Well, if you ever do, just sit in the ocean for a couple of hours. It works great for about two days."

I had just arrived in Dubai after along eighteen hours from Dulles to Amsterdam and after an eight-hour layover, I was in Dubai. I just checked into the La 'Meridian hotel by the airport where I was scheduled to be for two days before I was to go in country to Kabul. I was in the Lobby Bar when I met Ralph. He worked for the same company I did and was on leave to decompress from being in Afghanistan. It turned out, we were going to work in the same office.

Ralph was in his mid-fifties and had been in the Middle East and Asia for over twenty years. He had worked in India, Turkey, and Indonesia. He was later chased out of Saudi Arabia for reasons he wouldn't explain. On his continuing quest for a crisis, he landed in Afghanistan. He had graduated from an Ivy League school with a degree in accounting. He later explained to me people, particularly accountants, don't understand the meaning of "bean counting" until they have worked in Ethiopia.

He was about six feet tall, skinny legs protruding out of knee-length khaki shorts with an enormous gut draped by a Hawaiian shirt. To accent his wardrobe, he was wearing fluorescent orange beach sandals and round sunglasses after the fashion of John Lennon in the late sixties.

"Then, after a night of boozing and whoring, it's back in the ocean. Hey barkeep! Gimme another whiskey!"

"How long have you been in Afghanistan?"

"About a year. I used to work for the fucking Peace Corps as a Budget Analyst. I just got tired of the effervescence and naiveté of these kids who had good intentions but no clue how the world really works. The Corps would give some briefings, but not a gun, and then throw them into the worst third world shit holes on the planet and tell them: 'You got a year, have a meaningful time.' Then, when they finished their year, if they lived, they would go back to college, become assistant professors and lecture with authority how every problem in this world is the result of American lack of insight or inaction. I finally decided I had heard enough of their leftist bullshit so I took their lead and left." He lit a cigarette, took a sip of Bushmills and smirked. I could tell his thoughts were going way back.

We were watching a bunch of European International Aid workers who had recently come back from Afghanistan. They were drinking beer and singing, feeling good about being alive. "What is happening in Afghanistan is not unlike a chemical process called 'Cross Linking.' You see those relief workers over there? They're working in absence of a basic concept." Ralph was mildly intoxicated.

"I think they are trying to help."

"It's the West's approach, Did a lot of musing."

"Amusing? As in being entertained by their efforts?"

"No. Musing as in thinking about what they are trying to do. When we meet up in Kabul. I'll introduce you to a lieutenant who is far more effective in helping people than these oversized charities are."

"So what basic concept is missing?"

"What's going on in Afghanistan reminds me of a lecture I was forced to listen to in Organic Chemistry. It was about 'Cross Linking.' I need another drink to see if I can remember it."

"I thought you were an Accounting major."

"I was, but I needed something easy to graduate. Hey, barkeep!" He took a slurp, stood up and announced to the bar, "Everyone listen up! I just had a profound thought that you might want to hear!" The Christian Aid workers stopped singing and looked over.

Ralph held his drink in the air and declared, "History is being made in Afghanistan. It's called Cross Linking. That is a secondary set of reactions that link natural and synthetic polymer chains together. These reactions are generally different than those used to prepare chains initially of any fiber but may be similar or the same when reactions to conditions like heat pressure and chemical exposure are different or more severe such as high temperature, tension, and chemical treatment, which the Soviet Union and Iraqis have been known to do." He paused and took a swig from his glass. I was fascinated. The guy was clearly on a roll. I asked him if I could use his lighter. It was an old Zippo made out of stainless steel and had an engraved circular logo on it for a Irritable Bowel Syndrome Support Group. The chapter's name in the middle was: FART. I lit a smoke, leaned back on the bar and enjoyed everyone in the room watching Ralph. I didn't know if this was his bar humor or if he was serious. He toasted the Aid workers, lit another Lucky Strike and continued, "As a result of those reactions, the substrate or individual chains act less independently and more like a network. Cross Linking is a finishing step, while in many cases improves performance in end use applications, provide better strength and chemical resistance. It may also limit end use applications by making the finished product less flexible. The process is less flexible and others are improved. On the human side, there is generally only one opportunity to get it right and the results will be studied for good or ill afterward. Take those thoughts to Afghanistan." The Aid workers applauded. He sat down and continued talking to me privately. I finished my drink, put my glass on the bar and said, "Ralph, you are full of shit."

"Ha! Hey, barkeep!"

"Ralph, having spent many years working in this part of the world, and in Africa I think there is an urgent need to help."

He looked over at me and said, "Having wasted many year in Africa trying to help a bunch of people that are basically cave men, I came to the conclusion that charity is a racket. Think about the U.S. Government's AIDS relief in Africa. What a dumb shit idea. Trying to help dysfunctional people is a waste of time and these relief efforts have established an industry tugging at people's heartstrings. Reminds of when I was a kid in New York City watching the Salvation Army collecting around Christmas. They collect money from people that can't afford it, peel off a slice, and give the remains to people who don't need it, because they are going to die anyway. Think about it. The President wants the U.S. taxpayer to cough up six billion dollars to buy condoms for people in Africa that don't know how to use a pencil, much less a condom. You can buy a lot of condoms for six billion dollars."

He lit another smoke, exhaled and said, "Too bad they won't be used."

The guy had me intrigued. He obviously didn't work for Doctors Without Borders.

"Ralph, think about any relief effort. It's an effort, not necessarily a solution. I think at the end of the day we will be judged not by results but by our intentions and efforts. It's better if you try to achieve something that doesn't always happen but as humans we have to make the effort."

He looked at me incredulously and said, "That is the dumbest thing I have ever heard."

"We'll find out at the end of our days."

He lit another Lucky Strike and said, "That Arab woman over there has a nice ass. You want another drink?"

"Sure."

Ralph looked at the woman and took a drag on his cigarette, I knew what he was thinking. She did have a nice ass. "What are you doing in Kabul?"

"I'm trying to establish a financial system for the Afghanistan National Army."

"So how is that going?"

"It's hard to do without a banking system and none of the soldiers in the army of Afghanistan want to accept Afghan money. There is also a culture of taking what you can get when it presents. A good example was last week, we sent eighty thousand U.S. dollars to the National Bank of Afghanistan in Harat. The money was intended to pay the salaries of the Afghan Army troops in that region. It took a five-vehicle convoy with two fifty-caliber guns in the lead and rear vehicles and seven point six two chain guns in the middle. The money was in two-foot lockers. The manager signed for it. The American soldiers risked their lives getting there and back. Only problem was: The next morning, the bank manager was gone and so was the eighty thousand."

"So, what's your approach?"

"Keep trying. The best you can do is to try to teach them. You got to understand, there were, and still are, despite what the official line is, six tribes controlled by six warlords. Their pay was what they could steal. After the American invasion, Karzai came to power and decided to create a normal nation, which is unusual around these parts. He decided, with a bit of Western arm twisting, Afghanistan needed to establish a National Army, which was a creative thought considering a real army in Afghanistan has never existed. So, he made all the warlords generals. Took them out of tribal dress and provided them with uniforms."

I looked at him incredulously and said, "That's the dumbest thing I ever heard." I paused and asked, "Are we making progress?"

"Yeah, for the time being. But I will tell you, as soon as the world turns off the cameras and the Americans go home, things will turn back to where it used to be. The only difference is: We're training them to American army standards. The warlords will have the best trained, best equipped, most disciplined tribes with a professional officer corp. First time in history of

Afghanistan they won't have to fight on horseback or with a pickup truck cavalry. It's all about the poppies in the West and the Silk Road in the South." He was kind of drunk but I found his insights interesting and invaluable.

"Hey, Ralph, | am going to go to bed. it's been a long trip from Dulles to an eight-hour layover in Amsterdam to here. Let's get together for breakfast in the morning and talk more."

"OK. You get some sleep. I'm going to get some pussy."

"Nicht Schlafen!"

Breathing is getting harder. . . keep going. . . Don't quit!

After twenty-two years in the Air Force dealing with young enlisted folks, I had to deal with all manner of problems, usually they were self-inflicted. The small percentage of Airmen couldn't have been more creative in figuring out ways to get in trouble. The next morning when you asked the offender what happened, their answer was always, "Nothing." I was amazed at the categories of crimes which were described as nothing. As I watched Ralph making his way toward the Arab woman, even though he was older and should know better, he had the potential of creating nothing. Thankfully, he was not my problem. On my way out, over my shoulder I heard, "Hey bar keep! Gimmie another whiskey!"

The next morning as I was having a cup of coffee and reading the *International Herald Tribune*, Ralph plopped down at the table. He looked as if he was paying for the night before. He was dressed for the occasion. He was wearing knee-length purple shorts, a fluorescent yellow Hawaiian shirt with pink flamingos as the theme, beach sandals and cheap dark sunglasses. He looked like something you would put on the top of a water tower to keep aircraft from hitting it.

"Come on, follow me. There is a bar by the pool that's open. I need a Bloody Mary."

As we were walking around the pool with the cloudless sky and brilliant sunshine, we passed a European tourist laying on a lounge chair by the pool. He was about five feet, nine inches tall and weighed about three hundred pounds wearing an international orange Speedo. As we passed him, Ralph stuck out his arm, pointed his index finger and bellowed, "What the hell is that!?"

We sat at the pool bar and Ralph ordered a Bloody Mary, I ordered a Screwdriver. It is the same thing as a Bloody Mary only made with orange juice. We both took a sip from our drinks and I looked at Ralph and asked, "Do you have Asperger's Syndrome?" The syndrome is modern medicine's latest diagnosis for explaining why some people are socially retarded.

"Not that I am aware of."

I took a sip of my Screwdriver, amused because you rarely find people that honest.

"So, your year is about over. What are you going to do next?"

"I have a sister in Washington who is sick and about to enter a hospice. I think I probably should be there when she croaks."

We both took sips from our drinks. The morning sunshine was brilliant, dancing off of the water. "Got anything lined up?"

"Not yet. But if you can't find work in D.C., you are unemployable. I don't have any doubt about the future. I'm just not looking forward to it."

"Why? After a year of Afghanistan, I would think you would look forward to the break."

He lit another cigarette and snapped his lighter shut and said, "The whole Federal Government and corporate scene back in the States disgusts me." He was looking at the fat man in the chaise lounge and continued. "We got a generation of kids that are willing to commute two hours in each direction to sit in a cubicle all day, high five each other when the office gets a new copier or software. Their whole lives are based on one and zero, not people or places. I actually heard a conversation between a 'mentor' and these kids rating about how much cheaper it is to buy sateen ties than silk. That's why I left. It made me want to puke.

He took a drag on his cigarette and followed up on his thoughts, "In the sixties it was flower power. When it was over you took off the tie dyes and moved on. In the seventies it was disco. When it was over, you donated all those clothes to the Salvation Army. That's why you see so many homeless people looking like John Travolta. In the eighties it was making money. Some did, some didn't. In the nineties and until now, it's the extreme generation, the tattoos, body piercing, and extreme sports. You know why all that shit exists? They are trying desperately to add something to their lives. What do they expect. They have been brainwashed into thinking a meaningful existence is to work in a cubicle and get a tattoo. They are missing something intellectual and fun in their lives. They are incapable of thinking ahead of themselves. It's just full tilt boogie because they are so goddamned bored. The irony is: There is nothing intellectual about doing something extreme. The industry of the future is when all these people grow up and move on to another fad and want all their tattoos removed."

He took a sip of his Bloody Mary, lit another Lucky Strike cigarette and continued. "When I see a commercial that exploits the bullshit expression 'think outside the box,' it makes me wonder, 'what are you doing in a box in the first place?' The word 'box' is the digital generation code speak for a cubicle. The whole environment is so fucking stale, they have to have 'off sights' to communally figure out what to do. Anytime you need a group to make a decision, the result is going to suck. You know what the real basic zero and one is? The zero is the barrel of a gun and the 'one' is the bullet leaving it."

I finished my Screwdriver. There was a pause in the conversation and while I didn't disagree with his basic concepts I finally said, "Ralph, maybe you should stay here."

"Could be an option."

"Nicht Schlafen!"

Come on, breathe…

The German language cast my memory back to when I was a boy growing up in Giessen, Germany. My father worked for the U.S. government and he had rented a beautiful house across the street from what the locals called "Swan Lake." The house had a descending driveway which was about eighty feet long. The yard had many apple trees and I have many wonderful memories of picking the large sweet green apples.

There were so many apples and my mother didn't want to waste one of them. We had apple pies, apple sauce, apple juice, apple butter, etc. My father once told me when we were alone that he was afraid to take a nap on the sofa because he feared my mother would stick an apple up his ass. There were so many, my father and mother would host apple picking parties. All of their friends would come by the house, enjoy some appetizers and German beer and wine and pick as many as they wanted. The only rule was: Bring your own bags.

One day, my mother decided the gardens needed color.

She wanted a contrast to the beautiful emerald green that is Germany in the spring. She decided to plant long stem red roses from the front door all the way to the gate. Often, coming home from school, I would come through the gate and find her kneeling in the rose beds wearing a wide-brimmed straw hat, tending to her flowers. She and they were beautiful.

"Nicht Schlafen!"
Breathe . . . push . . .

As I lay on the treatment table gasping for air, I thought about my wife Anne. | met her when she was a young captain and a resident physician in a Family Practice Program in Washington, D.C. One night, on those few occasions when she had a night off, over dinner in a wonderful Georgetown restaurant, we were reminiscing about our families and growing up. I told her a story about when I was a six-year-old boy, I got into some kind of trouble. I don't remember the specifics but was eavesdropping on my parents conversation and remember my father saying the age-old phrase to my mother: "Don't worry Betsy, Edmund is the type of person who can fall into a pile of shit and come up smelling like a rose." I never mentioned that to my wife for the next twenty-two years.

"Nicht Schlafen!"
Inhale, exhale, inhale, exhale . . .

Many years later, I was stationed as a major and later promoted to lieutenant colonel in Italy during the Balkan War and was working as the Regional Logistic Director for the Air Component of the Southern Region of NATO. Anne and I rented a villa in northeastern Italy in the country between the villages of Iutizzo and Gorizzo. The closest larger town Condroipo. This was Italian white wine country. Behind the house there were over two thousand acres of vineyards.

The villa was situated on about five acres of planned and well-maintained gardens with a driveway about one hundred and eighty feet long enclosed by a ten-foot-high black iron fence and gate which had spear points on the top of each vertical member. I could open it with a remote control device which I kept in the glove compartment of my car. Part of the rental agreement was I was to pay the gardener who had been working there for twenty years. He maintained the grounds and they were immaculate. His name was Secondiamo and he had a particular passion for roses.

Outside the front door, there was a triangular rose garden. Secondiamo had established a wonderful garden of long stem yellow roses. Typical of Italian houses, the villa was not air conditioned. During the summer, we would open the windows in the front and rear of the house to allow a breeze. Many nights when they were in full bloom, the house was filled with the fragrance of roses. The only downside to roses are the thorns. I discovered this by accident coming home from Slovenia with pneumonia. My thoughts were bouncing and again I wondered: How did I get here?

"Nicht Schlafen!" The nurse was shaking me by the arm. As I tried to breathe, I thought of the Aid Station on Camp Eggers.

"*Any history of lung disease?*" The question evoked a memory.

I thought back to when my wife and I had been working in Europe for many years. We decided at the beginning of our European excursion we were going to celebrate New Year's Eve in every European capital. Due to the number of years we had been there, we were running out of places to go. Then, the Iron Curtain dropped and opened up new possibilities.

At the time, we were living in our villa in northeastern Italy. We were sitting by a fire in which the hearth was constructed in the round surrounded with upholstered benches. It was unique to the Friuli region of Italy, being so close to the Alps, not only for warmth, but also to cook. I used the cropped grape vines that came from the vast expanses of vineyards behind the villa. Secondiamo used to collect the wood and stack it against an old barn behind the house. One night in November, it was bitterly cold. I lit a fire and had it roaring. The smell of the burning grape vines, some as big around as your arm, were popping and producing the most comfortable heat. We were both sipping chilled white wine made from the vineyards in the back. I asked: "What do you want to do for New Years?"

"Ljubljana. It's one of the few capital cities we haven't been to. Since the end of the Cold War, there are a lot of places we can go."

She was thinking about Cold War rules when both of us were Air Force officers with security clearances and couldn't travel to certain places unless it was official business. Once the wall dropped, we could go where we wanted.

"OK. You make the arrangements.

"Nicht Schlafen!" I was doing a pirouette through space. *Come on; squeeze!*

Two days after Christmas, we were driving to Ljubljana. The weather was bright, clear sky and cold. From where we lived, Ljubljana was only about a two hour drive north. I could see the Italian Alps at about the eleven o'clock position with snow on the peaks. Anne was driving because I was feeling very tired. The country was beautiful as we approached Trieste. After we crossed the border into Slovenia, it was a remarkable difference. The Cold War was over but what remained in what used to be the East was distinctly twenty years behind what we were used to. It reminded me of what Germany was like when I first went there as a boy in the early sixties.

We stopped in the town of Postojna. It was known for its caverns with unique prehistoric salamanders. A local entrepreneur offered boat rides through the flooded Postojnska Jama cavern. My wife and daughter wanted to take the short boat trip through the cave. I told Anne I didn't feel well. They went to take the tour and I stayed in the local café that was just outside the entrance of the cavern. I entered and saw a fireplace with a warm fire burning, I chose a table next to it. Each table had a single red rose in a small Italian Grappa bottle. I was not interested in beer or wine but I do like to try local things, I ordered a regional drink called Crystallizer Koum-Kouat Vassilakis. It is bottled in Greece and is vodka in a bottle full of kumquat clippings. Quite different, bordering on disgusting. After one, I switched to coffee.

"Night Schlafen!"
My heart was racing. Try hard. Breathe.

After about an hour, Anne and Allison appeared and we continued our trip to Ljubljana. We passed scenic villages and wonderful landscapes and entered the city. Due to my miserable sense of direction, Anne was driving. I never understood how she could do it, but if you put her into any strange city on earth, she could find where she wanted to go. We approached the city from the south and proceeded down one of the main boulevards named Slovenska Ceta. We found the hotel on the left, pulled up to the front and unloaded our suitcases. While I was checking in, Anne was parking the car. As I was filling out the registration card and providing our passports, the registration clerk asked: "Have you been to Ljubljana before?"

"No. My wife and I thought this city would be fun for New Year's Eve."

He smiled broadly and said, "It is." Then, he put a small wine glass on the desk, reached under the counter produced a bottle and poured a shot of Crystallizer Koum-Kouat Vissilakis. He said, "For the New Year and the future."

"Nicht Schlafen!"

I can make it. Inhale, exhale . . .

We left for dinner at nine in the evening. The restaurant was named the Pri Sv Florijanu. It was a very quiet, peaceful place. There was a string quartet softly playing Vivaldi. I ordered a three course meal of veal, fish and dessert. Anne ordered a meat kabob dinner. We shared a bottle of Slovenian wine. After dinner as we were sipping a digestive, Fernet, I asked, "Day after tomorrow, what time do you want to leave?"

Anne looked at me astonished and asked, "What are you talking about?"

"There is a war in Bosnia. Things are about to happen that I don't want to discuss here but I have to be back on the second."

"Well, I'm on leave until the fifth. I thought you were too."

"Honey, we obviously have a huge misunderstanding. I have to be back on the second. Best way to solve this is for me to take a train back and you and Allison can tour the area. I'll be home when you get back."

After dinner, we put on our winter coats and made our way to Preernov trg, the central square in the heart of the city to watch the fireworks. The Franciscan Church of the Annunciation and the statue of their national poet Franc Presern were both highlighted with lights. The pink cathedral and the granite statue seemed to be a fitting center of gravity considering the swings of the pendulum of history the country had endured. The square was crowded with groups of friends, each person had their own bottle of champagne or wine. Tiny snowflake were falling and there was a trace of snow on the ground. When the church Mass was finished and people were spilling out of the cathedral, the fireworks began. With every boom, crackle, thud, and pop, a cheer would rise from the crowd. Bottles were raised, hugs and kisses were exchanged. I remember thinking it was a wonderful celebration of life and the future. Optimism and hope were clearly in the air.

New Year's Day was cold and overcast. I went to the train station to check the schedule for my trip back to Codroipo. I had to change trains in Trieste to move on to Udine. From there I had to catch a milk train which would stop in every village on the remainder of my way home. It was going to be a long day. After buying the ticket, I met my wife and daughter in a café across the street from the station. It was noon and I had about two hours to wait. Anne ordered a Coke and my daughter was sipping milk. I ordered a local beer. We talked about my urgency to return and the Balkan War.

Twenty minutes before the scheduled departure, we paid the bill and walked across the street to the train station. My train was on platform three. I had a hang-up bag and a small leather bag that I used to carry my toiletries, underwear and socks. I tossed the bags on the train, gave both of the girls a kiss, and boarded. I put my bags on an overhead rack, pulled down the window and waved to Anne. She shouted, "I'll call you when I think you're home!"

As the train slowly departed the station, the wind picked up. It was a cold crisp dark afternoon. I closed the window, pulled a book out of my leather bag and started to read.

"Nicht Schlafen!"

Inhale, exhale, inhale, exhale . . .

The train ride home was not the most direct route. Departing Ljubljana, the next major stop was Trieste. When I arrived in Trieste main train station, I put down the book and watched the people from all over Europe leaving and boarding the train, rushing with the determination they were going somewhere or going home. From there, on to Udine. When I arrived, I had a one and a half hour wait for the milk train to Codroipo. I took my bags to the landing and carried them to a café that was at the end of the railhead. The café had the typical stand up tables, about chest high for people who were just passing through. I dropped my bags and ordered an espresso and a small cheese pastry. I felt exhausted and didn't know why.

As I was standing there drinking coffee, about twenty feet away there was a Serbian man with bird cages. He was trying to sell the birds to anyone who was trying to catch a train. It was one of the best examples I had ever seen of poor marketing: Why would anybody catching a train, handling luggage, want to buy a bird? I suspected at the end of his business day, he took them home and ate them.

The ride from Udine to Codroipo was uneventful and very slow as it stopped in every small village along the way. I was the only passenger in the rail car and was reading the entire way. I was forcing myself to stay awake so I didn't miss my stop. That part of the trip seemed to take forever. When I arrived in Codroipo, I stood up as the train was coming to a stop. I felt a pain in my chest. I didn't think it was unusual considering I had been sitting in the same position all day. I collected my two bags, got off of the train and walked through the station to the front where there was a traffic circle and the taxis waited. I was the only human being in the train station. As I walked out of the station I thought, *Almost home.* I looked around and there wasn't a person or a vehicle out there. Then it hit me. This was the evening of the first day of the New Year.

"Nicht Schlafen!"

Breathe, do it. Keep thinking, keep working . . .

I had no other choice than to pick up my bags and walk home, which was about three miles away. I walked about five hundred yards to the town center. I needed a rest. My favorite place Café Centrale was closed but there was another around the corner. Because it would be on my walk home, I checked to see if it was open. It was. I usually didn't go there because the lights were so bright you needed sunglasses. It was the only café open so I stopped. The café reminded me of the Hemingway short story *A Clean, Well Lighted Place*. I put down my bag at the bar and ordered a Sambuca. I was breathing heavily and was thinking about the rest of the walk. It was a moonless night and pitch dark outside and I knew as soon as I left Codroipo, it was going to be hazardous. There were no sidewalks and I was going to have to walk carrying two bags on a two lane country road which was perfectly straight where Italian drivers would open up to speeds exceeding eighty miles an hour. There was an occasional car racing down the road and I knew the last thing the driver was expecting was a pedestrian carrying two suitcases. Whenever I heard the noise of an engine or saw headlights, I would step down into the ditch that was about five feet deep on each side of the road. I finally arrived at the villa and was staring at a twelve-foot gate made of iron with spear point on the top of each vertical member. Normally, I would open it with a remote control. While I had the keys to the house, I realized the remote control was in the glove compartment of my car which I could see in the distance. I put the suitcases down and decided: The only way I am going to finally get home is to climb that gate.

There were two horizontal members equally spaced which I used as a ladder. I climbed to the top one, swung my left leg over and thought: I'm wearing wingtips with leather soles. If I slip, I will be impaled and nobody will find me until sunrise. Once

I was over, I opened the house and pushed the manual gate button and retrieved my bags. On the way to the front door, and due to the asymmetrical weight of the bags, I tripped on a paving stone and landed in the pruned roses. I walked in the door, dropped the bags and pushed the button inside the front door to close the gate. I went into the kitchen, rinsed the blood off of my arms and poured a shot of Jack Daniels. I swished it around in my mouth, spit it into the sink and inhaled the vapors. I could hear my lungs crackling. Standing there trying to breathe, the phone rang. "Hi, Ed, I thought you would be home by now. How are you doing?"

"I can't breathe."

"Well, go to the clinic first thing tomorrow and get a chest X-ray. I'll call the internal medicine doc when we hang up and let him know you're coming."

"What happens if I die tonight?" I asked jokingly.

"Then you won't have to get a chest X-ray in the morning."

"Nicht Schlafen!"

Breathe, breathe. Keep trying. God, please make it stop.

After Italy, I was reassigned to Arizona where my wife and I bought a house. I missed the fragrance of the roses of Italy so I decided to plant a rose garden. Arizona is the perfect climate to grow roses if you water them enough. In fact, the largest rose bush in the world is in Tombstone. You have to pay an entrance fee to see it but it is well worth the trip. The rest of Tombstone is a place where 1800 people who don't want to live with the rest of the world hide out.

When we left Arizona we moved to Maryland. I had just built a home and decided, after the roses of Italy and Arizona, to grow roses as a hobby. The journey to Afghanistan started with a phone call while I was dead heading my roses in the garden I just established. The Vice President for the International Division of my company asked, "I got a job open in Afghanistan, do you want to go?"

"Nicht Schlafen!"

Don't quit, breathe, breathe . . .

Trying hard to avoid falling asleep, I thought of my introduction to Afghanistan. Two days after meeting Ralph, I was on an Afghanistan Airline flight to Kabul. With the exception of a goat in the back of the passenger cabin that went berserk on takeoff and landing, a result of a change of cabin pressure, it was a routine flight. When we landed in Kabul, the symphony began. There was the usual cacophony of the Islamic world. For many cultural reasons, there are no orderly lines there. Until then, I thought the worst two were Morocco and Turkey, but Afghanistan far surpassed any absence of civility I had ever encountered. It was all pushing and shoving.

The goat was still pissed off and was head butting people. His owner had tied a rope around its neck and was desperately trying to drag him away from the crowd. It didn't help that an Afghan man who looked like a trainer for Al Qaeda was hitting the goat with a walking stick. In that part of the world if you are predisposed to be passive, you won't get to where you want to go. There, people are only polite to people they know.

Don't quit, breathe, breathe . . .

I was flushed out of the airport to a large traffic circle which served as a pick up and drop off point. It was similar to a very slow merry-go-round with the outside cars and donkeys moving clockwise and the inside moving counter clockwise with someone occasionally making a U-turn, all honking their horns or shouting. All manner of vehicles from donkey carts to Ukrainian busses were parading by. There was a Chinese Army truck painted blue with benches on the bed. It was probably stolen. It had Chinese writing in white letters stenciled on the tailgate. I found out later it stated, "The Right and Righteous and Higher Human Transport Company." The noise and the dust added to the welcome.

Mark Twain once wrote, "History doesn't repeat itself, but it does rhyme." As I was standing outside the terminal, a local entrepreneur approached me and wanted to sell me a dove. It was in a cage made out of grape vine. My eyes have always been overly sensitive to light in the early morning. The morning sun was almost overpowering. The merchant's opening pitch was, "You want?"

Squinting, I said, "No."

"Please, make very good cat food."

"In case you haven't noticed, I don't have a cat."

"OK, for you my friend, I lower price to two dollars."

"Get lost."

"Nicht Schlafen!"

Concentrate, breathe. In, out, in, out. Staying awake is getting harder.

An American approached and asked if I worked for my company. I said yes. He introduced himself and we exchanged greetings. He then explained he was going to take me to the Safe House where I was going to live for the next year. He had two Afghan men with him. He turned to them and said something in Dari, the Afghanistan language very similar to Farsi. They both started picking up my bags, a year's worth of stuff, dragged them across the circle and began loading into the back of a van.

There was another guy who was also expected. An ex-Marine captain. He left active duty after being assigned to the Pentagon working in Military Investigations. He was going to work with a staff with the goal of establishing an Inspector General Office for the Army of Afghanistan. In the United States military, the Inspector General is charged with investigation of all matter of offenses, financial or personal. I thought, as he was explaining this to me, having worked in this part of the world for many years: *Good luck, you will need it.*

We loaded up and started driving. As we were moving through Kabul I was looking out of the window of the van. Our handler explained the original name of where we were going to live was the White House but some army officer decided, based on our lifestyle and to honor the classic prison movies, to name it the "Big House." Because it was simple to remember and not speaking very much English, all of the drivers knew where the "Big House" was. So much for a secret "Safe House."

"Nicht Schlafen!"

Concentrate, breathe. In, out, in, out.

On the way to our accommodations where we were to spend the next year, the driver was negotiating his way through a traffic circle full of pedestrians and animals. I was looking out the left and on the corner saw a shop that had a giant sign which read: "Afghanistan Mathematical Center for Metaphysical Research." In the windows of the first floor, which probably was once a carpet store, there were highly detailed and excellently drafted large engineering drawings of astronomical depictions of the stars and bodies in the heavens. All the mathematical calculations were presented on the various displays. As many times as we drove by there during my stay, I ever saw anyone there.

"Nicht Schlafen!"

Come on. Breathe, keep going. Don't die, keep going.

We had entered the heart of Kabul. I was looking out of the left side of the van. We passed a small park where children were playing and the men were smoking and the women wearing burkas were watching their children. What struck me were the roses of every color. They were wonderful considering how dreary the city looked. They were the only color in town. I thought, *Why do I have to work so hard to grow good-looking roses?* These are unattended and looked great. Maybe death seeps into the soil and pushes up miracles.

There were very few cafés but there were numerous kiosks cooking kebobs and flat stone cooked bread, vegetables and bottled water. There wasn't any charcoal or wood so they used anything they could get their hands on. The fires produced the most foul green and yellow smoke that blended into the haze of Kabul. An Army Occupational Medicine doc later told me they did some studies and found out that ten percent of the particles suspended in the smog was the dust remains of dead animals or people that were always in the road somewhere in the city. Dust to dust. We passed the mosque for that part of the city. It was the largest building around, soon to be surpassed in height by a modern glass office building that was being constructed across the street. I wondered: *Why would anyone build a modern glass building in Afghanistan?* One block down, the driver turned right onto a side road and we approached the Big House. There were four Afghan guards with AK-47s standing in front of two twelve-foot high gates. The driver hit the horn and the guards slid a gate open and we drove into a parking courtyard.

The Big House was a white nondescript modern-looking four-story building. From the parking courtyard facing the front, there was a fountain that didn't work and next to that there were five steps up to the front door. At entry level there was a veranda. To the right of the entrance, there was another veranda with a door which led to one of the apartments. The entire first floor had sandbags stacked four feet high around the building. There were balconies for the apartments on the second floor to the fourth floor.

Our bags were unloaded and taken to the lobby. It was a dark but very comforting. When I passed through the main doors, I entered a shadowed, beautiful place. It was a hall made of marble with stained glass on the windows on the back. In the middle of the room, there was an eighteen-foot highly polished table that had carved walnut around the edges. Sixteen matching chairs surrounded the table. Our Program Manager was sitting at the table with our personnel files in front of him.

"Welcome to the Big House!" He looked at me and said, "You are Air Force, twenty-two years." He looked at my partner and said, "You are Marine, sixteen years. I'm Army, twenty-four years."

The Marine looked at him and asked, "You got any room in the Inn?"

"We have two rooms available. Both are on this floor. Everyone wants to live on a higher floor because this one is the most vulnerable. You guys are new so you got 'em. As people leave at the end of their contract or get killed you can move upstairs and the next new guys will start here. We have two rooms. One is in the back left end and one is on the front right. The good part about the back left is it's larger and safer because the only view is a wall of a building across the alley. The room on the front right is smaller but has an adjoining kitchen and bathroom. The downside is it faces the gates and the street. Any car bombs go off you will get a glass shower."

The ex-Marine and I looked at the rooms. The Director asked, "Who wants what?" We both looked at each other. The Director pulled a coin out of his pocket and said, "Call it."

I said, "Tails."

The Marine said, "Heads."

He tossed the coin in the air and it landed on the marble floor, bounced twice and finally flopped over. The three of us bent over and looked at it. The Marine and I, having never seen an Chinese coin, asked in unison, "What the hell is it?"

The Program Manager looked at it, squinted and declared, "Not sure, but I think it's heads." While we were studying the coin, an Afghan houseboy appeared and saw us bending over, staring at the coin on the floor.

The PM looked at him and asked, "What is it?" The houseboy looked at us as if we were idiots.

He said, "It is a coin."

I was assigned the room on the front right. It had sandbags stacked halfway up the glass picture window and door which opened to a marble terrace that had never been used. On the inside of the glass was a dark film similar to what is used to darken automobile glass in the United States. It was applied to minimize the effects of explosions. I peeled it off. I didn't care. I was not going to live in a cave for the next year. I opened the door to the landing and faced four feet of sandbags. I had to go out of the front entrance of the house and climb five feet to the landing to remove the sandbags in front of my landing door. The room reminded me of an oversized old hotel room. It did have a fresh coat of white paint. It was furnished with an oversized single bed, night stand, mahogany desk and chair, and plenty of closet space with drawers on the bottom third.

From the landing outside of my room, over the clay pots with a single rose plant, I could see the parking lot where the drivers would start to gather about five-thirty in the morning. We would leave at six. They would take different routes and drop us off at the first gate of Camp Eggers, the U.S. Army Headquarters for Afghanistan. On the way home, we crossed a busy four-lane street to the parking lot of another safe house called the Alamo. The drivers that brought us to Camp Eggers were always there. They knew our routine and were willing to drive us to any location we requested. The company I worked for had leased the vans from India. It didn't matter if the driver's station was on the left or the right, the sliding van doors were always on the left. I always carried a geology hammer on my right waistband because traffic drove on the right. If I was blown on its side I could get out. The automotive glass used in India will not shatter like American car glass. You couldn't break it with your fists. The idea of burning alive was frightening.

"Nicht Schlafen!"

Breathe . . . Damn It! . . . Breathe . . . I feel like I'm sinking.

There were two dining facilities on Camp Eggers, one was called "The Rose," the other was called, "The Goat." We were having breakfast at "The Rose" one morning which we preferred because it was near our office. It was called "The Rose" because of its abundance of roses surrounding the building. The food was plentiful and quite good but "The Goat" had a better selection. In the dining area of the Rose, there was a big screen TV which would show delayed soap operas broadcast from the Armed Forces Network coming out of Germany. All the army soldiers and marines were engrossed in the storyline of *Days of*

Our Lives and would make a point of watching every episode. If they couldn't see it, they would catch up by discussing what happened with someone who saw the latest episode they missed while they were on watch. Each table seated eight and there were gun racks at the end of each one. We would go through the line and when finished, randomly sit at the first available seat and discuss the interesting items of the day.

I was sitting across from Ralph and there were six other people eating. They were talking about a soldier who was killed the day before when his vehicle slid off the side of a mountain in the south of Afghanistan. An Army Major who was eating biscuits with creamed chipped beef gravy said, "What a dumb way to die: Inattention."

Ralph offered his opinion in his typical booming voice:

"Shit happens. I read a story a few years ago in the *International Herald Tribune* about some dumb ass German zoo worker who was taking care of a sick elephant. The elephant was constipated, and after giving it mega doses of laxative, he decided to disimpact it. So he gets behind this animal full of shit and starts to dig. Then BAM! The beast cuts loose. The force of the explosion knocked him flat on his back and when the back of his head hit the concrete floor, knocked him out. The elephant proceeded to shit all over the guy from his waist up. About three feet of shit covered his entire torso all the way over his head. I think the official cause of death was: He either inhaled shit or swallowed it."

We were all sitting there with our forks suspended in air between our food and our mouths, we all stopped chewing. The Major was staring at his biscuits smothered with creamed chipped beef.

"Somebody shoot that son of a bitch!"

Everyone at the table ducked. We thought the intended target was Ralph. It turned out, it was a soldier caught up in

Days of Our Lives. The voice was shouting at a character in the soap who was playing the asshole of the month.

"Nicht Schlafen!"
Take a deep breath, in . . . out.

After breakfast, I would always make a point of taking two turkey sausages to a cat who would visit our office twice daily, sometimes more. We were sitting in our office and the cat was on the window ledge. Jim engaged the office with a heart-tearing discourse about the plight of some Afghan families he discovered. He was the most foul-mouthed guy I ever met but he had a heart of gold. He graduated from Boston College with a degree in Accounting. He and Ralph were a team when it came to all aspects of the Army of Afghanistan's financial affairs. He was not a big man, but with his fiery red hair and penetrating blue eyes, he captured everyone he talked with. He was passionate about certain things, particularly helping people. Jim was talking about his efforts to help ten refugee families who were living in a bombed-out warehouse on the outskirts of town. He discovered them by accident and was immediately taken by their plight. The families had fled Afghanistan when the Taliban came to power and went to Iran. Once the Taliban were removed by the American invasion, they heard life would be back to normal so they returned to Kabul. Each family had about three children. Jim told us about the miserable existence they endured: "Last winter, it was so cold, they burned their shoes to keep warm. Biggest problem now is there's raw human waste flowing out on the street and these kids are walking in it barefoot. I have got to figure out a way of providing proper toilets."

I was sitting at my desk working and monitoring the conversation and at that point, I turned my chair and remarked, "Don't even think about portable toilets. Someone will have to pay for them. And even if you can find them, you won't find a company that can empty them." I thought about the writings of William Blake, "The greatest sin is ignoring the impulses of one's heart."

"What about slit trenches?"

"Not in this culture. That works in the field where there are only men."

Stewart was reading the latest edition of the *Stars and Stripes*. It is the official military newspaper for the troops that has its history going back to World War Two. It is one-third stories from the wire services, one-third human interest stories, of that no human could possibly be interested, unless they had their biweekly pointless death story. The final third was the most popular, the sports page. We all knew Stewart was a CIA officer. He never admitted it and we never asked. He was a Columbia University graduate, fluent in Dari, and a sponge for information. I thought it was amusing when the translators would return our documents, he would always ask, "You want me to proof that for you?" He also would disappear for five to ten days at a time and when he returned, would sit at his desk with his feet propped up and read whatever newspaper he could get his hands on. He slowly put his newspaper down, smiled and asked: "Are you expert in shit holes?"

"Yes Stewart. I'm a Registered Engineer for Disaster Relief with the Royal College of Engineering in London. I'm quite familiar with shit holes."

"London?"

"Not at all. London is one of my favorite cities. The Royal College of Engineering simply certified I can recognize a shit hole when I see one and I know how to build one."

I turned to Jim and said, "There is more than one way to skin this cat. There are many options available." The cat on the window ledge basking in the sun lifted his head, looked at me and said: *Excuse me?* I looked at Jim and said, "There are ways to solve the problem."

"*Thank you.*"

"I think the pour-flush method would work. The engineering is simple. It would provide privacy, almost no odor, and no flies. It's basically a modern toilet over a covered pit. Next to the stool you have two buckets of water. When you finish, you pour one bucket into the bowl and use the other bucket for hygiene. You know in this culture they don't use toilet paper. That's what the second bucket's for. The toilets can also be positioned where there is no line of sight between the men and women."

"Seems to me if you have to go real bad, it wouldn't matter if someone saw you entering a latrine." Lieutenant Commander Don West was an active duty Navy officer sitting at his desk clipping his fingernails. He was a Naval Academy graduate who was into bodybuilding and diet supplements. His job was to work on force protection issues and advise the Iraqi military due to his training as a Navy Seal. He was new to the office, had never worked in the Islamic world and was learning "the ropes." We each had a translator assigned to us to translate what we wrote into Dari. All of them were Pakistan University graduates who had left Afghanistan during the rule of the Taliban. When we wrote a document we would give it to them in English and they would translate it into Dari. When they finished, they would bring it back written in Dari and would read it to us in English. One day the officer's translator came in with a twenty-page document and proceeded to read it out loud. The Commander parked his feet on his desk, put his hands behind his head and listened.

Part of the paper was about the details of force protection. One part was how to set up defensive positions. The topic was "field of fire." That is military jargon for describing how to cover a piece of ground with gun, rifle, and cannon fire from two or more directions. His translation was: "Your crops are on fire." LTC West dropped his feet off of his desk, pulled out his pistol, snapped off the safety, cocked the hammer and said: "Don't make me use this." The translator bolted out of the room. We all looked at him. Jim was the first to speak. "We know you are new here and that was an attempt at humor that I thought was kind of funny but you have to think about what these people have been through. During the Taliban they would have been shot for screwing up a translation. He didn't know if you were serious or joking. You need to understand: Here, life means nothing." We all turned back to our desks and continued working.

"Anybody got an empty Coke can?"

Later that day I looked out of the window by my desk and saw West and his translator on our concrete bench sharing a bag of dates. The officer was showing his translator how to break down and reassemble his pistol.

"Nicht Schlafen!" As I was gasping for air, what kept me trying was watching her nipples pronounced on her surgical scrubs. I remember thinking: "*Darling, I'm not going anywhere . . . come on push!*"

My thoughts returned to Camp Eggers. An Army Captain came bursting through the door. The guy was a very skinny officer who would run ten miles every day on his twelve hours off. We got so used to seeing him running by our office windows we collectively decided he was nothing more than a second hand on a clock. "Who wants to sign up for the 4th of July Fun Run?"

Ralph was sitting at his desk drinking a bottle of water and was the first to reply. "What's fun about running? I'm not interested because I don't have a death wish. I believe every person is born with a death sentence. We are given a finite number of heartbeats. What makes life interesting is, you never know how many you have left. I have no intention of using up what I have faster than is necessary." He pulled out a Lucky Strike and said, "Hey Mason, you want to go out for a smoke?"

We both got up and on our way outside pulled a bottle of water from the refrigerator. Ralph took two. We sat down outside on a concrete bench in the shade under a large trellis supporting a huge series of grape vines. The leaves were so large, they provided perfect shade from the blazing Afghan sun. Ralph lit a Lucky Strike and I pulled out a chocolate from a British tin that I had purchased in Dubai. As we were sitting and smoking, we were watching our gardener. We were fortunate to have one of the few offices with green space outside. He was cutting the grass with scissors. I thought, *he might be the Research Director of the only "Afghanistan Mathematical Center for Metaphysical Research."* After about thirty seconds of watching him work, Ralph walked over to him and gave him a cold bottle of water. He put his right hand on his heart and said, "Thank you." Ralph came back and sat down and lit a Lucky Strike.

I asked, "What's wrong with a lawn mower?"

"The Army won't give one. Here, gasoline is limited. All the vehicles are multi-fuel so they use diesel. Besides, he is being paid forty bucks a month and has no timetable to get this grass cut. He is a nice man trying to support a family of six. That's why the office, every Friday, we all kick in five bucks apiece and give it to him before he goes home. Don't try to talk to him. The only English he knows is 'Thank you.' You'll also notice every Friday at sunset, he will be leaving out the side gate with flattened cardboard boxes he collected from the dumpster behind the Post Exchange. That is what his family will sleep on for the next week."

"He looks like Osama Bin Laden."

"Yeah but he's not tall enough. Osama is six ten. But he looks so much like him we have had conversations in the office as to when someone was going to shoot him by mistake."

"Pick 'em up and put 'em down!"

I looked to my right and saw Don leading two Afghan men, one carrying a sign with a post and a bag of quick dry concrete, the other carrying two shovels, a level, and two liters of bottled water. Coming down the walkway, he had them marching in step. The procession marched onto the grass and Don with his command voice said: "Plant it right here!" The gardener looked up briefly as if he was trying to figure out what was happening. He decided it wasn't a threat to him so he continued cutting the grass. Don sat down on the bench.

I looked over and asked, "What the hell is this all about?" The two Afghans were digging a post hole. I looked at the sign laying on the grass. It read: "Do not shoot. He is not Osama Bin Laden."

"Had the Army Engineers made it. Don't want anybody to kill him or we will have to do this ourselves. Besides, this will make a couple of good bullet statements in my FitRep. Saving the life of a citizen. Maybe a medal." We were watching them finish the hole and they started pouring a bucket of water in it. Don bellowed, "Hey shitheads! Post first, then mix the concrete in a bucket and place it in the hole. I want that post vertical. I showed you guys how to use a level. Use it! And after you got it in there and true, one of you guys hold that post for thirty minutes until the concrete sets!" He took a swig of water, looked over at us, grinned and said, "There's got to be something true in this country."

The gardener who couldn't read English walked over and looked at the sign, turned to us, put his right hand over his heart and said, "Thank you."

After about thirty minutes, Don addressed his forces. "OK, good job, guys. You can go. I'll call you when I have more work."

Ralph looked over and asked, "How are you going to call them?"

"The way things were done before cell phones. Open the window, stick your head out and yell at 'em."

As we settled back into our desks, an Army Major came storming into the room. He was livid and focused at Bill who worked for another contractor and was managing vehicle issues. The Major demanded to know exactly how many ambulances were going to be delivered to the Afghan army. We all looked at him as if he were an alien. Stewart, with his feet on his desk, reading his newspaper, seemed unaffected. The cat on the windowsill looked up and yawned with the sunshine flowing over him through the window.

Bill was the guy who knew every aspect of vehicle acquisitions for the Afghan army. He was a contractor for a different company than mine and didn't have a dress code. He wore jeans and custom-made cowboy boots. He was a University of Texas graduate in Information Systems but wound up working vehicle issues because the guy who was doing it before him had been blown up. Because we couldn't smoke in the office, he chewed tobacco. He constantly had a wad in the side of his mouth and would, after about six chomps, spit into an empty Coke can.

Bill spit into his can and said, "Fifty-six."

The irate Major exploded. "Then why do I keep reading we have one hundred and twenty on order? How can I build an army if I can't get the right information?"

Bill spit into his can.

He knew the answer but based on Major's approach, decided to drag the conversation along. We were all drinking coffee and smirking, made eye contact with each other and mentally connected: He was singularly going to build the National Army of Afghanistan? After a long pause, Stewart slowly lowered his newspaper and calmly stated, "Hey, Dickweed. There are two types of medical response vehicles for the Afghan army. One is a Battlefield Response Vehicle which is used to extract casualties from the field. The U.S. military doesn't use them because we have helicopters. They don't. The other medical vehicle is an ambulance which is used to transport patients. Bill just told you 'Fifty-Six.' Do the math."

The cat began licking his butt fifty-six times. Bill spit into his can, leaned back in his chair, propped his boots on his desk and asked the ceiling: "Why does this sound like something I wrote two weeks ago?"

4

"Nicht Schlafen!"

Inhale, exhale . . . try harder . . . the sun should be up soon.

Abruptly, Colonel Horne came rolling through the door. An Army Colonel, he was about six feet six inches. His presence was larger than his stature. He was a Citadel graduate with a pronounced Southern accent. He didn't know it, but we used to refer to him as Foghorn Leghorn. He had the same strut, the same body language, the same accent, the same self-confidence, and the same last name. The cat ran like hell.

"I say, it makes me glad to see all of you fine officers are gathering like this and having a professional exchange of ideas." He was on his daily rounds and probably heard the conversation from outside.

Suddenly, a U.S. civil servant came walking through the door. "Hey, guys. I am here on a temporary assignment from Army Material Command trying to explore the possibility of establishing the concept of Configured Loads for the Army of Afghanistan. I heard you guys were supply folks so I thought I would come by and introduce myself." He was a retired Army Warrant Officer, that is basically a glorified Master Sergeant and had achieved some perceived stature in Civil Service, probably GS 12 or below. It was obvious he had some kind of cosmetic surgery, probably to have bags removed from under his eyes. He looked like an owl. Colonel Horne turned, smiled and asked,

"Why haven't you had the courtesy to come by my office and introduce yourself?"

Before he could answer, Stewart slammed the newspaper on his desk and said, "We are not supply folks. We are advisors to the Government of Afghanistan." I sat up straight, feet on the floor, turned my chair and said, "Let me help you. I am very familiar with Configured Loads."

Configured Loads were initially developed by the U.S. Air Force as a way to re-supply medical units in the field. The system would provide exactly what was required, when it was required. It took the U.S. Army a few years to figure out it was a good idea. The army application is if you are a captain in the field, and you need to build a two-man defensive fighting position, rather than ordering each component piecemeal, i.e. barbed wire, 2x4s, sandbags, and a host of other things required to construct one, you only ordered one thing: A Defensive Fighting Position. Everything you needed to build one would be on one pallet. The key to making it work is velocity and precision. The army still hasn't figured that out.

"In Afghanistan, a Configured Load is what you can load on the back of a camel or throw into the back of a Toyota pick-up truck."

"Ha! I'll let you men continue your professional discourse. Mr. AMC, come see me when you learn something from these fine officers."

"Anybody got an empty Coke can?"

About ten minutes later, a new Colonel came crashing into the office. He had a document in his hand that authorized the transfer of three thousand Meals Ready to Eat, or what the U.S. Army calls MREs, to the Army of Afghanistan. He demanded to know, "Who authorized this?"

I looked at the signature block on the form and replied, "Lieutenant Enswim." While I never met the guy, I knew there was a lieutenant that was heavily involved with the orphans of Kabul and I suspected he was Stewart's creation. I also knew he was risking his life and career to help them. "Two weeks ago, he transferred eight hundred." We smiled. The lieutenant had flawlessly delivered his second load of food to the orphans. The Colonel demanded to know where he was. "I've checked the processing section and they have no record of a Lt. Enswim."

Bill spit into his Coke can and remarked, "The guy is a logistical genius."

Stewart lowered his newspaper and commended, "Aristotle wrote 'Excellence is not an Act but a Habit.'"

He looked over at Bill and asked, "Where is he getting the trucks from?"

Bill spit into his can and replied, "Beats me."

The Colonel turned, glared at me and demanded, "Where does he work?"

"I don't know."

"Who does he work for?"

"If I knew that, I would know where he works."

Stewart lowered his newspaper and said, "I think Lt. Enswim is in trouble." Then he smiled, winked his right eye at me and remarked: "If you can find him." The Colonel stomped out and slammed the door.

Tom, glued to his monitor, remarked, "Now I know why he wanted to borrow four trucks last week." He looked over at Stewart and winked his right eye.

I was scanning the room and said, "At the end of the day you will be measured. Lt. Enswim's scale is continuing to tip in his favor."

Bill spit in his can and asked, "You want to be the office chaplain?"

Ralph looked over at me and said, "Hey, Mason, let's leave early. I'm tired of this bullshit."

"Nicht Schlafen!"

Don't quit . . . come on . . . breathe . . . God this hurts.

Across the street from Camp Eggers was a parking lot in front of a safe house we called the Alamo. The parking lot in front was the area where our vans waited. To get there we had to cross a busy street. The traffic was fast, bumper to bumper, and there were no pedestrian crosswalks that wouldn't have meant anything anyway. There, life was nothing. Trying to find a break in traffic, I thought about the day before when I had a meeting with an Afghan General. He was most gracious; his orderlies served diced watermelon and dates with tea in his office. We discussed the business at hand and the conversation eventually turned casual. Through the course of discussion, I mentioned I originally graduated from university as an architect. His eyes lit up and he said: "Come. There is something you might be interested in."

He made a call on the intercom and we left out of his private entrance. Out the door a four-man security detail was waiting and we got in his car. Two guards were in the car ahead of us and two in a car behind us. We drove to downtown Kabul to the Grand Boulevard, parked on the sidewalk across the boulevard where there was a massive construction project in progress. An enormous mosque was being built that would rival the size of any cathedral in Europe. He explained it was funded by the government of Saudi Arabia. The architecture of the building was beautiful. As I was admiring the structure, the general took my arm and said, "Colonel, watch this."

The boulevard was four lanes and heavily trafficked. Thirty yards away a man was attempting to cross the street. He was dressed in local garb. He was in the stance you would expect to see in a track event in the Olympics. Suddenly, he hiked up his robe and made his dash. He was immediately creamed by a bus. The General had his security detail stop traffic in both directions and we walked over to the man. A British Army doctor who looked like David Niven walking on the other side of the boulevard also witnessed the event. He walked over to the man, knelt down, put his hand on the man's throat, gingerly lifted his head, inspected both arms and legs and pronounced, "He's dead." The security detail dragged him off the road so traffic could keep moving. There, life meant nothing.

Carefully, looking both ways, Ralph and I made it across. Once on the other side there was a parking lot full of mini vans. The most striking feature of the van pool was the tent. The drivers had managed to get their hands on a white tent that had large stenciled letters on it which read: UN High Commissioner for Refugees. It was probably stolen. The tent was erected in the gravel of the parking lot used for our van pool. Inside, they had oriental carpets. They used the tent to get out of the sun, nap, eat, or pray while they were waiting to take us back to the Big House. We were early and they were not expecting us. Ralph flipped open the flap of the tent. Two of the drivers were in the middle of their prayers. Ralph bellowed, "Which one of you assholes is going to take me home?"

I looked at Ralph. "If you keep doing this, they really will take you home."

"Nah, they're being paid more than most people in this country."

"That's still no reason to interrupt their religious practices."

"Fuck them. I want to go back and take a nap."

"Ralph, maybe when your tour is over, you should pursue a career in Waste Management."

As we walked to the van, there was a blue one and a half ton Chinese army truck in the parking lot. It was painted with the familiar Chinese letters on the tailgate. Who knows what they were up to. As we were getting into the van, Ralph was staring at the truck and announced, "I once had a profound thought."

"Twice? What was it?"

"Don't know. I wrote it on a bar napkin, stuck it in my pocket and forgot about it." He lit another Lucky Strike, snapped his lighter closed and continued. "Two weeks later, I put the same pants on and went to the Big Day Bar." He was referring to the Chinese whorehouse and restaurant about half a block from the Big House. "I started sneezing repeatedly so I pulled out the bar napkin and blew about a pound of snot on it. Between the mixture of the snot and ink, it all mixed together and I lost it. What I learned was, you don't write profound thoughts with a fountain pen on a paper bar napkin."

"Too bad. You could have been the next Plato."

"Nah. I'm not a queer." He leaned over to one side, cracked a fart and lit another cigarette. I think Plato would have stroked his chin and had deep reflections about the meaning of Ralph's existence.

"Ralph, you ever thought about dying?"

"No. That's a given. What I have thought about is when it's going to happen."

"It will be the next time you fart in the van."

"Nicht Schlafen!"

This is getting hard, concentrate, breathe . . .

It was Friday and we were having breakfast at "The Goat." We were there to eat and kill time until the market outside the gate opened. You never knew when that was going to happen as all the merchants had to set up and be ready for business before the U.S. Army brought the bomb dogs through and cleared the area. The Goat was probably the safest place to have breakfast in the world. At the end of each table there were the usual rifle racks. Everyone was armed to the teeth. As Ralph and I were moving through the food line making our selections, Ralph, in his signature loud voice exclaimed: "No self-respecting raccoon would eat this shit!"

"Ralph, the food here is not bad."

"True. But it sickens me to be cooked food and served by creatures who look like their last job was a baggage handler for Greyhound."

"Maybe you ought to think about working in a cubicle. Less human interface."

"Could be an option."

Friday was our only day off as it was the Islamic Holy day. It was the only day when we could wear anything we wanted. Normally we were expected to present a professional appearance dealing with the level of Afghan government we encountered on a daily basis. I met up with Ralph and he was wearing a pair of blue jean knee-length shorts, white socks, red sneakers and a tee shirt that had a logo on it that stated, "I Do Not Exist."

The market was cleared and Ralph and I started browsing. I was standing in front of a table that had helmets which the proprietor was trying to convince any American soldier who passed by that they were original helmets from Genghis Khan's armies. At closer inspection, they were actually Soviet Army helmets left over from the war that had metal wings welded on to the sides and all manner of ornaments welded all over the top. They looked OK for a Hollywood movie, but hardly real. Ralph was negotiating with a vendor at a nearby table.

"I have absolutely no intention of giving you money for that piece of shit!" He was arguing about a replica, advertised as an original missing parchment page of the Dead Sea Scrolls. I walked over to the table and asked, "Ralph, are you trying to start a riot?"

"No. We have had this conversation every Friday for the last year. Sooner or later, he'll drop the price. It's a test of wills. When I wear him down enough, he'll cave."

"Do you really want it?"

"No."

"Nicht Schlafen." The urgency in her voice was waning.

Don't quit, breathe, breathe . . .

The vendors sold all manner of things, some real, but mostly fake. There was a merchant with a display you would encounter when you cleared the last ring of security for Camp Eggers. He sold antique British Army rifles. What he would tell the young soldiers shopping was his rifles were captured when the British, after many years of occupation, attempted to retreat through the Kyber Pass and were wiped out by the Tribes of Afghanistan in eighteen forty-two.

In the days they were manufactured, British rifles were all made with the Crown of England stamped on the firing chamber. Under the King or Queen's Seal each rifle had a serial number stamped on it. Each British soldier who was issued a rifle had to memorize its serial number. The problem was the Enfield rifles had the serial numbers stamped upside down. Upside down or right side up, does it matter to someone who can't read English or know Western numbers? It all looks the same to them.

As I was entering the market, there was a group of young U.S. soldiers shopping and holding the rifles. I stopped, thinking, *For these kids, this is their first time in this environment, let me help them.*

"Do you guys like these?"

One replied, "Yeah, they're pretty neat. They're old and have a history. They don't cost too much either."

"There is a reason for that."

"What?"

"They are not real. Look at the steel plate on the firing chamber. It's called a lock. If the weapon number is stamped upside down, and it doesn't specify the city in England where it was made, you know it was made here. Afghan and Pakistan gunsmiths, like their American counterparts, were quick to recycle parts as it was much easier to restock a gun than to build parts from scratch. Locks were also exported by lock makers for overseas gunsmiths so they could be from salvaged parts or installed as new. The only thing British about these rifles are the locks and even they should be suspect. Do you think the King or Queen of England would allow that inattention to detail to arm their army at the height of the British Empire?"

The merchant was enraged and was glaring at me. We made eye contact. I calmly put my hand on the grip of the pistol in my shoulder holster. He smiled and turned to the soldiers, and said, "OK, I give you half price."

"Nicht Schlafen!" I didn't know how much longer I could last.

This feels as if somebody is standing on my chest.

The reason I was there was to buy a vest, which is a necessity in Afghanistan. I saw a merchant who sold all manner of clothing. He had canvas vests. There were probably four hundred identical vests on clothes hangers at the stand. All of which were different sizes, not displayed according to size. I was looking for a khaki vest with many pockets. The reason you need them is to carry all manner of things, from insect repellent, passport, shot records, money, maps, and ammunition. I told the vendor I wanted a medium-sized vest. He took one randomly off the rack and handed it to me. On the label in the back of the collar, it was marked XXXL. I tried it on and it was as if I was wearing a trenchcoat. I told him I wanted a medium.

He took the vest, turned around and faced the rack of vests, paused for about three seconds, turned back around with the same vest and said, "Here a medium." I realized, in order to find the right size, I was going to have to try on all four hundred vests he had on display because the only labels he provided the women who were sewing the vests were XXXL. Because they could not read Western text, much less Roman numerals, they would just sew them in there, regardless of the size of the garment. I wasn't going to waste all day trying them on. I thanked him and left. I was thinking of all the bazaars I have stopped, this was hardly unusual.

I have always been fascinated by ink wells. They are symbols of literacy and civilization. I started to collect them years ago and I have looked for them in antique shops, markets, and bazaars everywhere I have been, from England to Morocco to Turkey. The most interesting one I have found was in Marrakech. Anne and I were walking through the noise and bustle of the market hours just after sunset. That is the time when commerce begins because nobody wants to go out in the heat of the day. I passed a stall where an artisan carved camel bone. He had all manner of things but what struck me was a two-canister inkwell carved from bone of a camel foot, gracefully held together by silver straps. It had silver lids and two reed pens attached to the sides of the wells. I bought it.

The merchant looked at me with a smile, absent of many teeth and said, "I will wrap this for you if you give me a cigarette."

Inhale . . . try . . . don't quit.

I continued through the Kabul market looking at the tables. There was one merchant who had displayed all manner of brass and steel objects. There were bayonets from France, England, Russia, and just about any Western power who ever set foot in Afghanistan. There were candlesticks and incense holders but what caught my attention was a brass inkwell which looked like a daisy. It was a brass flower with the center as the main basin for black ink and all the petals had lids and opened to contain different colors. It was one of the most unusual inkwells I had ever seen.

"How much for the inkwell?"

"I could never sell it. It belonged to my grandfather. He brought it back from Uzbekistan many years ago." Ralph rolled his eyes and said he was going to the tent that sold clothes. I turned back to the merchant and asked, "So, why are you putting it on the table?"

"You have to have honey to attract bees."

"No. Here, you have shit which is attracting flies. How much?"

"Twenty dollars, U.S. I do not want Canadian."

My negotiations were interrupted. Over the noise of the market, I heard a familiar voice a few tables down bellowing. Once again, it was Ralph driving a hard bargain. He was at a custom tailor's tent which had a variety of suits ordered by soldiers who never picked them up. The market was only open on Friday and many soldiers would put half down with the understanding they would pay the balance when they picked up their order. A couple of days after the transaction, they often would get orders to leave. What the merchants had for sale were the remains of their customers' transactions. Ralph was trying to order a sport jacket. The merchant was suggesting high fashion in an attempt to reduce his current inventory of bell bottom pants with pinstripes that were horizontal.

"All I want is a god damned blue blazer in which I can meet with the assholes who are running this shit hole you call a country!"

"Very diplomatic, Ralph. Maybe you *should* go home."

"Could be an option."

We continued shopping and four tables down, a merchant had the same flower petal inkwell I saw earlier. I stopped and looked at it, toying with the petals. The merchant was attentive and asked, "You like? Very old. From Kazakhstan. It belonged to my grandfather."

"How much?"

"How do I put a price on such a rare thing?"

"How much?"

Ralph commented: "That son of a bitch must have been screwing everyone on the sub-continent. You think his name was Stan?"

"For you my friend, fifteen dollars."

"Put it aside. I'll be back later."

Another fifty feet, I came across the third identical inkwell. At that point it was becoming amusing. I looked at the merchant and said, "Let me guess, it is very old and belonged to your grandfather."

"Yes. He brought it back from Turkmenistan."

Ralph pulled out a Lucky Strike and lit it. He snapped his lighter closed, looked at me, grinned and said, "Stanley the Great was very busy."

Keep trying, don't quit, breathe . . .

We started walking to the Coffee Café and passed a vendor with just about every DVD known to man lined up on the ground on display. After shopping, we were sitting in the café, listening to an army female sergeant talking to a group of soldiers about how she had bought a DVD in last Friday's market. It was the Tom Cruise movie, *Mission Impossible.* I remember thinking, *that's appropriate.* She went on to explain that it was dubbed in a high-pitched voice speaking Russian. She told the three soldiers sitting with her, she didn't speak Russian so she shot it.

"Nicht Schlafen!"

Don't quit, breathe, breathe . . .

I thought of waking up every morning at about three. I enjoyed getting up that early because it was a perfect time to call my home in the United States. It was also comfortably dark. There was a nine-hour time difference and I knew my wife would be home. I also had to be at work by six. What I particularly enjoyed was listening to the call to prayer from the mosque about a half a block from our building. I had a kitchen with a coffeemaker which I would load the night before and would turn it on as I went into the bathroom. I would open the window which was just above the shower, sit on the toilet and listen to centuries of religious training. Sitting there contemplating the meaning of life and listening to the melodic chant from the mosque, I thought about all the Islamic countries where I had worked: Morocco, Tunisia, Egypt, Turkey, and now Afghanistan. I thought, *I was glad how it was working for, to have a real toilet. In that part of the world it's normally a hole in the floor. No wonder there was never a Reformation in Islam. They don't have a place to think.*

When I was finished, I was sitting in my brown canvas beach chair on the veranda just outside my door, drinking a bottle of water and looking at a crescent moon. The sandbags that were stacked halfway above the window to prevent blast damage was a favorite pathway for the cat who would make her nightly rounds. Ever since I was a boy, I always had a special affection for cats. They could communicate with me mentally and I would talk to them verbally. The cat, gray, brown, and white-striped, would appear when you least expected to make her nightly sounds. I would buy Vienna sausages from the Post Exchange and place a couple on top of the sandbags for her. She arrived on time as usual. When she discovered the sausages, sniffed for a bit and asked, "*What are these made of?*"

I answered, "I don't think anyone on this planet knows."

"*Are they well enough to eat?*"

"Sure, if you're hungry enough."

She decided to start chomping. As she was eating, I said, "A merchant in Morocco once told me that Mohammed would return in the form of a cat."

She had just finished her meal and was cleaning herself. She stopped, snapped her head up, looked at me and said, "*That is possible.*"

She paused and continued, "*This taste like dove.*"

As she was walking away, I asked, "Are you Mohammed?"

She stopped and looked back, "*Nobody knows.*"

I was sitting there drinking a bottle of water and smoking a cheroot, listening to the soft din of the generators in the distance. I was looking at the crescent moon and watching the safe house guards doing their shift change. I was thinking of the centuries of history that preceded me.

Suddenly, there was a crashing sound in my room and Ralph exploded on to the landing with his beach chair. It was similar to mine, constructed of wood and canvas. The canvas on his chair was a Confederate flag. I marveled, *Where did he get that in Afghanistan?* He plopped down and opened his bottle of water. I flicked my smoke into the parking lot.

"What's going on, Ralph?"

"I have been thinking about my toes."

"What have you discovered?"

"If you don't have any, you will have a hard time walking. Same for thumbs. If you don't have them, you can't hold a pencil or tie your shoes. You also can't hitchhike."

"I never gave much thought to appendages."

We were watching the guards change. I opened another small bottle of water and took a swig.

"What prompted the sudden interest in toes?"

"Do you remember the Army corporal from Mississippi who used to work the second level of security at Eggers, always had a big smile?"

"Yeah."

"He was in the field yesterday and had his right foot run over by a tracked vehicle. All of his toes on his right foot were crushed. I found out before I left work, they had to be amputated." He flicked his cigarette into the parking lot, leaned slightly left in his chair and let out the loudest fart I had ever heard. Good thing he got rid of that smoke before it happened.

I thought, *his whole life was filled with luck*. Eventually, explosive gas combined with Lucky Strikes will be his demise.

"Too bad. He told me he was on his track team in high school and when his enlistment was over, he wanted to go to the University of Southern Mississippi, study history and try out for the track team. He was a sprinter."

"Not anymore."

Listening to the morning prayer, Ralph commented it was too long and too loud. I looked at the cat and said, "It's the same as church bells, only a different octave. When you listen to their prayers, think about the church bells. People wonder why there are suicide bombers in this part of the world. During the Civil War, the South melted their church bells to make cannons. Sometimes humanity abandons their religion for what they perceive as a higher purpose." I stood up and poured the remains of my water on the only rose that was blooming on my landing.

"Nicht Schlafen!"

"Living on a prayer. It don't come easy" . . .

That evening I needed to wash my clothes and for some reason there were no house boys available so I decided to do it myself. I went down to the basement where the laundry room was available to all and loaded my boxers, socks, and T-shirts into the washer. Ralph's room was down there. The only guy living in the basement. Pretty smart when you think about it: Anything happens, he was going to survive. I knocked on his door, he answered and a cloud of smoke cascaded out of the room. Ralph was wearing a high neck white T-shirt and an old scarlet-colored robe that looked like he bought it from a Salvation Army store. His left hand was clutching a black Bible with gold lettering and a Lucky Strike was hanging out of his mouth. He looked as if he was about to conduct sunrise services for a bunch of city park winos. I asked, "What's up, Ralph?"

He slid a chair for me to sit on, plopped on the edge of his bed and said, "Just reading the Bible. There's some pretty gruesome shit in there."

"What is your sudden interest in the Bible?"

"Never read the whole thing."

I lit a cigarette, sat back in the chair and asked, "Learned anything?"

"No. You want a beer?" He tossed the Bible over his shoulder.

"No."

He pulled out a bottle and asked the walls, "Where is my goddamned church key!?" He found it in his desk, snapped the cap off and took a big swig. I was amused. I asked him if he ever read the Koran.

"Don't have to. Same document, different language. Old Testament, I mean." He took another swig of beer, lit a Lucky Strike, cracked a fart and smiled. We talked about various aspects of life. His primary focus was on pussy. The buzzer went off for my laundry so I left.

On my way out I told Ralph, "There's a place for you. See you in the morning."

The next day, as a part of my morning ritual, I was on the landing outside of the door to my room at three in my boxers drinking a bottle of water, leaning on the sandbags stacked in front of the window, I was thinking about the song, "Living on a Prayer." I was never a particularly religious person but I have a great respect for those who are. I didn't want to intrude on their religious rituals so I would watch from the shadows. In the moonlight the call to prayer from the mosque would start and the guards would unroll their prayer carpets, lay their AK-47 rifles beside them and would take turns praying.

I sat down on my canvas beach chair smoking a cheroot, drinking a cup of coffee and a bottle of water, looking at a beautiful crescent moon when she arrived. The cat was sniffing the top of the sandbags intently. I had forgotten to place two Vienna sausages out the night before.

The cat asked, "*Where are the sausages?*"

Out loud I said, "What makes you think I have any?"

"*Because you are one of the few that likes us. We rely on your kindness.*"

I wondered how often she ate. As I was getting up to get the food I asked, "Is there a cat god?"

She replied, "*No. There is only one God. I am a part of Him.*"

"Well, you have it figured out. Gimme a minute and I'll be back with the sausages." The next day, I went to the Aid Station. I never saw her again. I hope some kind person is helping her.

"Nicht Schlafen!"

We're halfway there . . . inhale, breathe . . .

I hoped for me and the good people of Afghanistan, we were. But then again, halfway in Afghanistan is over two thousand years. As I was standing in the dark my memory went to a conversation I had with a friend in San Antonio shortly before I started my Afghanistan excursion. We had been stationed together years ago in Europe. I was in town on business and I gave her a call. We met early the next morning for breakfast because she had to go to work. Her name was Annie Bocquit. She was beautiful and full of life, Victorian and dignified in the way she carried herself. She was a colonel in the Air Force, a physician and prominent in the Air Force medical community. A perfect lady and a fine officer. Due to our long friendship I was fortunate to be one of the few people that called her Annie. To everyone else she was Colonel Bocquit.

I had known her for many years and knew she was hard-working and dedicated to her profession and our country's purpose. When she arrived she was wearing a European forest green battle dress uniform, referred to as BDUs. Having spent over two decades in the Air Force, I had worn them since their inception. They were heavy which were designed to contain heat, developed for the normally chilly climate of summer and cold winters of Europe. I was amazed that in the heat of Texas and the safety of San Antonio that would be the duty uniform. I smiled and asked, "What's with the BDUs?"

"The Chief of Staff has decided this is our standard uniform until the global war on terrorism is over."

"Well, expect to be wearing those until you retire. We can't win a war on terrorism because we can't declare a war on an idea."

The waiter arrived to take our order. She ordered the buffet and I ordered rye toast with grape jelly, a side of bacon, and coffee. I continued my thought: "Remember President Reagan's war on drugs? Has anything changed? Nope. When the leadership in Washington came to understand you can't wage war against a social problem, they just stopped talking about it. Wars are waged against nation states. Terrorists don't have one. You can extract revenge but you will never kill their will. Same as drug dealers. You can send them to jail, but it will never end the problem. Americans want a quick solution for everything, catching the organization that destroyed the Twin Towers or finding Saddam Hussein's weapons of mass destruction. The simple solution is: Just declare war on it."

The guard had finished his prayers, picked up his rifle and the next one took his place. Centuries of worship were unfolding in front of me. You can't kill their will.

Sitting there enjoying the peace of three-thirty in the morning, I heard a commotion blasting down the street. A crowd of about twelve to fifteen Afghan men were chasing someone. "Open that fucking gate!" I knew it was Ralph. The guards opened the gate quickly and he dashed in. Outside the gate, a loud intellectual exchange transpired. I could hear rifles being cocked. Ralph climbed five feet onto my landing, out of breath.

"What the hell was that all about?" I handed him a bottle of water. He was breathing hard. I don't think he had run that fast since he was a kid.

"Heathens don't know what's funny."

He left through my room and returned about fifteen minutes later with his folding Confederate beach chair. He was wearing a shoulder holster with a pistol on top of his Hawaiian shirt. He looked at mine and said, "Check yours. We may have company." He lit a Lucky Strike and snapped his lighter closed. He looked at me in the moonlight and smiled as if he had just accomplished something of great importance.

"Ralph, if you keep doing this they really will take you home."

"Ha! The only thing that's going to civilize this shit hole is a sense of humor. After all this country has been through in the course of its history, I think they should discover one of the most basic human pleasures: Laughter."

"One of the most basic human pleasures? Is that why you go to that Chinese place? To laugh? Have you ever heard the expression: Laugh yourself to death?"

He lit another Lucky Strike, blew a plume of smoke at the heavens and asked, "Ever thought about exorcize?"

I took a sip of coffee and asked, "Exercise? You mean as being chased around the block by an angry mob?"

"No. I'm talking about the removal of evil spirits."

"As being possessed by an evil spirit?"

"Yeah."

I took another sip, puffed on my cigar and wondered what he did in the Chinese restaurant and whorehouse to prompt his lightning dash home and those deep thoughts. "No Ralph. In my opinion, possession doesn't happen. It's all control. Evil can't possess anyone. When evil visits, you have complete control over it. It's the same as an unwanted guest in your house. You can politely show 'em the door or if that doesn't work you can say: 'Get the Fuck Out!'" We sat and smoked for a few minutes in the dark and, thinking about the Chinese restaurant and whorehouse, I had to ask, "What is your sudden interest in exorcism?"

"I bought *The Exorcist* on DVD at the market the other day just to bring back memories."

"Your college days must have been a hell of a lot of fun."

"The DVD had some good visual images but the problem was, it was dubbed with a high-pitched Russian queer voice."

"Let me guess." I took a drag on my cigar and blew it at the moon.

"You shot it."

"Did you hear it?"

"No. I was probably in the shower."

"Nicht Schlafen!" The nurse looked tired. She turned and walked out.

Keep breathing, keep going, don't quit.

As the sun was rising, I had to urinate urgently. The treatment tables had a cup holder on the side with a half-liter plastic bottle intended for that bodily function. I took off the oxygen mask and stood up on the left side of the bed and relieved myself. It felt as if I were breathing under water. The Dutch soldier was watching and when I finished, he said: "Please help me."

"What . . . do you need?"

"I have to void."

I thought that was an interesting word selection considering he wasn't speaking in his native tongue.

"Sure . . . I'll help." I asked, "Are you a physician?"

"No. My father was. He taught me English. Are you?"

"No. My wife is."

He looked at me in pain and said, "Please help."

I took his bottle and held it for him as he rolled on his back and said, "Thank you." When he finished he rolled on his back and said, "Thank you." I climbed back onto my treatment table and put the mask back on. I could hardly breathe. I was thinking how horrifying it would be to be that helpless. I was about to find out. One of the German nurses appeared and gave him an injection. What I was also going to find out, morphine, depending on the dosage, only lasts for about twenty minutes.

Inhale, exhale . . . Don't quit, keep going . . .

The Dutch soldier's condition reminded me of my wife when we were driving north on Route 1 up the coast of California and stopped for the night just south of San Luis Obispo. We were unloading the car at a beautiful seaside motel perched on a cliff overlooking the Pacific Ocean. The motel had thick, rich vegetation and the trees were illuminated. Anne, wearing sandals, slammed her foot into a landscape light and broke the big toe on her right foot. I remember the pain she had to deal with for months. I could only imagine what pain these soldiers were going to confront. I didn't know at the time, but what I had just done was an act of kindness that would be placed in the balance of my existence.

Deep, deep . . . inhale, exhale . . .

"I say, what the hell is going on here?" he bellowed. It was Colonel Horne stomping through the room. He walked over between my treatment table and the Dutch soldier and looked at me as I was struggling to reply. He said, "You don't have to talk, I just wanted to stop by to tell you, you are one of the few Air Force officers I ever met that wasn't a pussy!" I lifted my left arm and he took my hand with his bear-sized paw for about three seconds. I nodded and smiled from under the oxygen mask.

He was smiling, turned, looked at the Dutch soldier and said in a perfect Foghorn Leghorn delivery, "Whoa! Son, you need to pay attention to where you're walkin'!" The Dutch soldier smiled. I doubt if he ever heard of Foghorn Leghorn but the confidence the Colonel presented was infectious. The two German nurses were standing in the background and staring in amazement. I thought this was their first introduction to American bedside manner.

Try to breathe . . . concentrate . . .

As soon as the Colonel left, I was taken to an emergency room adjacent to where I had just spent the night. The nurses had been monitoring my oxygen saturation level all night. It was still 61 percent. A nurse put a pressure mask on me which blows air into your lungs. It was too tight on my face I kept lifting the mask using my right thumb and pulling the mask from my chin. The nurses, having stayed with me all night and compounded by the stress of Afghanistan, unloaded. After a tirade in German their message was: *If you don't want to live we can't help you.* It was one of the most powerful statements of the journey. Then they calmed down. They knew I spoke German.

One finally asked in English, "What is pussy?"

I lifted the mask for the last time and said in German, "Auf Deutsch . . . est heist Muschi."

They both started laughing and poking me playfully. Then, two European doctors arrived. One was Italian, the other was Slovenian. I was examined and the Slovenian doctor delivered his diagnosis in the typical bedside manner of a European doctor.

"I think you are in trouble."

Our Program Manager arrived to see how I was doing. He was followed by the U.S. Army Colonel who was in command of the Aid Station at Camp Eggers. The Colonel was pissed. He turned to our Program Manager and said, "I am so damned tired of you people diagnosing yourselves. If this shit continues, somebody is going to die!" I didn't realize at the time, it was going to be me. I remember thinking, *Jemand ist gerade über mein Grab gelaufen.* This is a German expression for impending doom. In German it means literally, "Someone just walked over my grave." A prophecy before you are dead and buried as what was to come.

There was the sound of a helicopter in the distance and becoming increasingly louder. It was coming in my direction. It landed outside. I thought more casualties were arriving. I didn't know it was for my long journey back. I was transferred from the treatment table to a field stretcher. The two nurses looked exhausted. Two heavily armed soldiers started to lift the stretcher when both exhausted nurses clasped my hands and said in German, "Got Mit Uns." Their eyes were welling up and I finally realized I was in big trouble.

"One, two, three, lift!"

Really hard now . . . breathe . . .

I was taken to the helicopter. My gun and two clips of ammunition had been removed earlier so I took off my shoulder holster and gave it and the keys to my room to someone. As I was being carried on the stretcher to the helicopter, I remember looking up at the cloudless azure sky of dawn in Afghanistan. The sun was about to peek over the mountains. I remembered the Ernest Hemingway book *True at First Light.* I thought about the sign, Don's smile as we were sitting on the bench, the gardener with his right hand over his heart thanking us for something he didn't understand. *"There's gotta be something true in this country."* As I was being loaded onto the helicopter with the rotor blades whipping around above me, my mind wasn't racing, it was slowing down. My peripheral vision went from normal left to right to looking down a six-inch tube. I remember wondering, *Why is this happening? There are no "G" forces in play.* A voice came to me and said,

"Yes there are. You forgot the other two letters."

Try . . . try to breathe . . . don't quit . . . push!

At that moment, everything went dark. The eight-week dream began. Somewhere during the flight from Camp Phoenix to Bagram Air Base, I found myself airlifted to a different place. It was my first step into an epic night journey through the heavens. I was going someplace else.

Part Two: The Eight Week Dream

"I have spread my dreams under your feet: Tread softly because you tread on my dreams."

—W. B. Yeats

7

Hiss, pop, snap, deceleration, thud.

I was confused. I had no idea what was happening. I was on a roller coaster ride, ascents, descents, and horizontal portions with hard right and left turns, ever increasing with velocity with an occasional violent stop. Each pause was a different location. To keep from falling out of the hospital gurneys, my wrists were restrained to their metal rails. I couldn't sit up. Struggling was pointless. The ride ended when I slammed into another cart in the parking lot of an old Southern grocery store. I wondered after looking up at the sign: *Is this going to be the measure of my life to expire in a parking lot of a grocery store?*

"They are shuttling us around because there is a war going on and they don't have the bed space. There are a lot of brave people that are in worse shape than we are. We are being moved from one hospital to another. That way nobody has to admit us and we move on. It's perpetual motion."

"How long . . . can this last?"

"For eternity."

The man next to me was an Army Special Forces Officer named Tom Morgan. I knew him from Camp Eggers. I don't know what circumstances brought us together in this predicament. I also didn't know what his injuries were and I didn't ask. A nurse stopped by to do something for him. When she bent over him, I noticed a pair of bandage scissors in her breast pocket. After she left, I looked at Tom and asked, "Did you see those scissors?"

"Yes."

"That is our key to . . . getting out of here. To escape. We have got to figure out . . . a way to get those scissors."

"Considering both of our hands are tied, what do you suggest?"

"I don't know. We'll figure it out. We can't . . . quit." I paused and continued. "Maybe, the next time she . . . comes by and bends over . . . try to take them with your mouth. She has large breasts . . . which causes the scissors to stand out . . . They are in her . . . left breast pocket . . . Just turn your head . . . and put your mouth on them and . . . take them."

We were laying outside of a loading dock. I realized this was a transfer point to the next destination. I was staring at the black night sky and watching a display of lights, not stars, much bigger than stars moving at random like a swarm of insects. Perpetual motion. A jerk of acceleration similar to the start of a carnival ride and we were off again to another place. During this leg of the journey, Tom and I got separated. I never saw him again.

As I was being moved from one medical facility to another, I was floating between a dream state and what was really happening to me. Often, I could hear everything and other moments I was in a different place. I was going to spend the night there and be moved in the morning.

Suddenly, there was a jolt of acceleration. I was quickly flying through a tube of beautiful colors, suspended in air, not making contact with the sides of the tunnel. There was a sudden deceleration and I landed with a thud. I was standing barefoot in soft deep sand, similar to what you would find on a beach, in front of a waist-high stone wall looking at a city on the other side. It was beautiful. There were no tall buildings. I looked in wonder at roses of every color and apple trees in abundance. The architecture was glowing in colors of dark yellow and oranges, and beautiful shades of green encased the surroundings. It was inviting me. I was tempted. There was a soft breeze in my face. The quiet peace was a sensation I had never experienced. Suddenly, there was a voice I did not hear, rather it came from inside of me:

"You have been weighed in the balance and you are welcome."

I looked at the city, the hard breathing was gone. I took three wonderful deep breaths before I replied. I didn't have to speak, just think, *"Thank you, but no . . . I am going home."*

I turned about and took two steps when the voice replied:

"As You Will."

As I was trudging through the deep sand, my first steps on the way back home, I wondered, *Was that a command or a challenge?* I thought, *Did you ever notice there are two l's in the words Will and Hell?* I had never been convinced about the concept of Hell. I was just starting to discover the similarities and differences between the two.

A young woman dressed in a white cotton gown appeared in front of me. Initially she didn't seem to be standing on the ground and there was a fragrance of jasmine in the air. She asked, "Do you have any idea of what you are walking away from?"

"I don't understand."

"Let me explain." She was standing on a large polished jade tile. She did a graceful pirouette. "Here is one state of existence.

But there are two states of existence. You haven't been shown the other. One is Light, One is Dark. To Ascend or to Descend. Ascension is a positive rebirth, to Descend is a negative rebirth. You have been offered Acension, do you really want to go back and risk the other way? Everyone is capable of imploding."

"I want to go home."

"It is all a matter of Will." She had the most charming smile. She turned and walked toward the city. As I watched her walk, the light from the city penetrated her gown and revealed the most graceful and beautiful nude female form I had ever seen.

Acceleration, ever increasing velocity, deceleration. Thud.

"Why is this man wearing a toe tag?"

"We are just trying to make it easy for you. When he dies, all you have to do is fill out the date, time of death, and sign it." I remember the hiss of the ventilation system, banging and clanging, and people shouting in the background.

"Take it off! You are too new to understand that half of this business is providing hope. You don't understand that this college humor can mean the difference between someone staying with us or slipping to the other side. Neither one of you realize he can hear everything we are saying. Life is not a joke. Is he prepared for flight?"

"Yes, Sir."

"He's waking up! He's fighting the restraints!"

"Check the bag, check the pump, check the line all the way to the IV."

"Here it is. The line was crimped." I was floating in and out of consciousness.

Peep . . . Peep . . . Peep. I kept hearing the constant chirping of a small bird. Peep . . . Peep . . . Peep. My vision was blurred but I could still hear everything.

I laid there and listened to three people discuss my fate. Another person appeared with a smile I recognized. It was tied to the gurney and could hear the ocean surf in the distance. Even though I was on a ventilator, I could detect the presence of salt water in the air. It was tropically humid. Laying on my back staring up at a streetlight I could see a cloud of fast-moving objects circling the light.

"He has obviously been misrouted. We don't have the capability to deal with him here. He's manifested for the next mission?"

"Yes, Sir." He bent over me, put his hand on the side of my throat and said, "Come on, buddy. If you don't quit, we won't quit."

I was rolled across the flight line toward an awaiting aircraft. I perceived the smell of jet engine exhaust and heard the din of an auxiliary power unit that provided electricity to the aircraft before engine start. There was a small tank of oxygen and a portable ventilator between my feet.

"He's feet heavy. Three on each side. One . . . Two . . . Three . . . Lift!"

I didn't know if I was dreaming or if it was real. I was carried up the back ramp of a cargo aircraft and my litter was snapped onto vertical stands erected in the middle of the aft end of the cargo bay. There was a clanging and banging and a flurry of activity. Even though I couldn't see, having been in the Air Force, I knew what was happening. I could hear the screw jacks closing the back ramp. The sound of four jet engines starting one at a time. The vibration of a huge machine preparing to hurl my body into three-dimensional space. Movement started with an increased jet engine rumbling, forward movement, breaking, moving again, and a burst of noise and velocity. I was on a ventilator and was moving in and out of consciousness.

There were two who were loaded ahead of me. One, a female soldier, was also on a ventilator and next to her was a soldier who was suffering from kidney failure. There were also about twenty ambulatory patients sitting in jump seats with various war wounds in the front of the cargo bay. After the take-off roll there was an instant cessation of vibration and an acceleration with the feeling of ascension.

After the take-off began, over the thunder of the jet engines I heard a commotion behind me.

"We got a problem back here!"

"Raise her head up!"

"I can't do it by myself!"

"You gotta reach a little bit higher!"

9

Acceleration, ever increasing velocity, deceleration. Thud.

I was sitting in a stone vaulted room at a mahogany table with a three-inch thick top. I was there as a contractor to the Cardinal of Doctrine and Policy for African Affairs to provide international logistics expertise to the Church for the ongoing African relief efforts. We were on an island in the Adriatic that was the seat of a Cardinal. I was given the only table available. It was in the doctrine and policy arena. There was no electricity so our light was provided by candles, two on each desk. The arched windows were open and it was sunset.

I could hear the soft Adriatic Sea splashing against the rocks and feel a soft salt breeze that would occasionally blow a candle flame sideways. A black cat perched on the window sill was silhouetted by the setting sun. At the end of the vaulted room there was a fresco of a person sitting on large rocks by the sea, head bowed and long hair half covering the face. I could see it was human but the features were indistinguishable. It was a human face that was in agony. Over time, the salt air had taken its toll and the fresco appeared to be in a fog. In the room were three monks and a nun who were working on documenting the actions of a knight who killed six and one half people during the last Crusade. They had access to the archives of the Church that contained old documents written in Latin.

Even though it was none of my business, I asked, "How is it possible to be one half of a person?" I continued. "If someone has both of their legs removed, does that mean he's half a person? If he loses the use of his arms and legs, does that mean he is a fifth of a person?"

The monk sitting next to me, smoking an unfiltered Italian cigarette and drinking an espresso calmly out his cup down in the saucer and asked, "How about if he loses his head?"

"Then he is dead. But he is still a person. His spirit will be decided elsewhere."

The monk sitting by the door, stroking his chin whiskers calmly added, "He's-ah right. We need to divine the definition of man." He looked at me and asked, "Would you write a draft of-ah those concepts so we can pursue those-ah thoughts?"

"No." My breathing was getting tight again. "For two reasons. First, I am here as a Logistician in an advisory capacity… The second and most important reason is that… I am not a Catholic and I don't think… it would be appropriate for me… to be involved in writing Catholic doctrine… that will last for a few hundred years." I leaned over on the table and put my head in my arms and tried desperately to breathe.

The nun came over and put her arm around me and asked if I was all-ah right. I told her, "I can't breathe."

She patted me on the shoulder twice and said, "It is possible you have just realized the idea you have given."

"I don't think… it is a new concept."

The cat on the ledge looked up, flipped his ears front and smiled. The monk sitting by the door dragged a chair across the slate floor, lit a pipe and said, "Perhaps you need-ah vacation. When we finish writing would you carry it to Bari? I will arrange to have someone meet you. There is good food there and many women."

"Yes, I will. For now, I need to lay down and sleep."

When I awoke, I was leaning on the deck rail of a two mast sailing ship with a soft leather pouch under my left arm. The pouch contained about twenty pages of parchment beautifully penned in Latin. There was a soft breeze coming from the port side and the Captain was tacking. I remember the sounds of the wooden ship groaning and the soft sound of the rigging stretching. We were approaching the old port of Bari. I wondered how the Captain was going to dock. This was clearly too large a ship to sail into port. The sails were lowered in a frenzy of activity. Two small motorized vessels approached and the deck hand threw out the lines and we were towed to the dock. After I left the ship I saw an old black Citroen with tinted windows and a priest leaning against the driver's side door smoking a cigar. He noticed me and approached.

"Mia scusa. Mister-ah Mason. I am Father Leonardo. You have something for me?"

"Yes. The Definitive Definition of a Man."

He smiled and said, "Doubtful. I know who is on the island. Come. I take you to a nice hotel with a beautiful café by the water. We eat some sardines and drink some wine." As we got into the car he asked, "Have you studied about the meaning of a human being?" The car started moving. The driver knew where to go. The Father had it all arranged.

"No. I don't have to. I am one."

He relit his cigar, looked over at me, grinned and said, "Profondo."

We drove up the Italian coast on a thin Italian road hugging the coast. The ocean was constantly present on my right. We stopped at a hotel where we were greeted as visiting dignitaries. After many hugs and handshakes, we were escorted to a terrace overlooking the sea. We were seated at a beautifully set table, white linen cloth, silver, and crystal, candles, and roses. The view with a full moon on the Adriatic was spectacular. I was introduced to three other priests and four women that were elegantly but casually dressed. I discovered through the course of the evening they were nuns.

The hotel was owned by Father Leonardo's brother. The hospitality was gracious and typical of Italian, uninhibited in conversation and comfort. We were served a seven course meal. All the portions were about the size of a large cup. The first course was a chicken consommé with two pieces of black bread. Tiny bowls of green and black olives in oil were placed as well as small sweet pickles in vinegar. Father Louis, a priest sitting across from me, opened the conversation. "I was told you were bringing the 'Definitive Definition of a Man.' Are you a messenger?"

"No. I am a courier."

"A prophet?" I could see he was having fun with the conversation. He was smiling.

"No. I am a courier."

The second course arrived. It was risotto with a clam sauce. The waiters produced chopsticks and placed them around each setting. I looked up at Father Leonardo and asked, "Why?"

He said, "My cousin is in conflict with the Chinese restaurant up-a the coast so he steals the chopsticks every time he can."

"Does anyone in Bari know how to use them?"

"No. But that's not-a the point."

A waiter appeared and poured more wine. The wine was flowing, changing with each course. The next course was cubes of veal in a butter garlic sauce. As we were working our way through the meal the discussion continued. Father Louis, smiled and asked: "I understand you were on the island. We have received the documents, I have read them but have not had the time to think. I would be interested to learn: What is your definition of a man?"

The fourth course arrived. It was a white fish cubed and baked with olive oil, garlic and oregano. I had a couple of bites, thinking about the weight of that question and asked, "Are you asking my opinion about the long history of Man or our present state?"

He looked at me as if he was going to explode. In typical Italian drama he demanded, "I need to hear!"

"OK. You need to understand my opinion is culturally skewed. To return to your question, 'What is the Definition of a Human Being?' Today, there is no being. Hire them and stick them into a hole. Today, people are the same as pegs in a wooden board game. There are no thoughts about life. In America it's only Monday Night Football and Thursday Ladies Night Out, as if you can find a lady in a bar on a Thursday night. The definition of a human being throughout history has been a long, loud groan." Throughout the conversation the nuns didn't say a word but at that point, they were smiling. The priest sitting next to him, Father Phillipo, chuckled and said, "How uplifting!" He winked at me and took a bite of fish, a sip of wine, and reached for a slice of bread. "You are starting to understand."

The next dish was grilled sardines, each about six inches long sprinkled with red pepper and doused with olive oil. A fresh loaf of bread arrived. Everyone was smiling. Father Marco, sitting next to me, looked over and asked, "Where did you study in seminary?" I was very tired and was growing weary of the religious banter. "In the Afghanistan Center for Mathematical and Metaphysical Research."

"I have never heard of this place."

"That's why it is so intellectually stimulating. Nobody has."

The sixth course was boiled shrimp with butter and saffron, simmered with thin sliced grilled beef. Father Louis took a sip of wine and said, "As much as the Church has always advised, I have come to the decision we are not all equal." He looked at me and asked, "Do you agree?"

"Yes. To a degree. I think what separates people is their Choice of Life and their Character which is in essence, Will. I think the measure of a man is by how he holds himself not when things go well but his comport when things do not. The two key words are Choice and Will."

The final course was a fresh salad with virgin olive oil. Fresh lettuce and sliced cherry tomatoes with ground cheese sprinkled on top. Father Phillipo looked at me and asked, "Did you ever notice the last is always the best?"

I replied, "No. I think the first is the most memorable."

The entire table exploded in laughter.

Father Phillipo took a sip of wine and asked, "How much did you have to do with the writing of-a the document?"

Hiss . . . sizzle . . . pop . . . snap . . . violent deceleration, heavy breaking, slowing . . . Thud.

I was laying in my back staring at the ceiling. A soft hiss of the air handling system was in the background. The room was cold, almost to the point of shivering. Two nurses were working on a counter with their back to me. I was restrained. An orderly entered and handed them a note. They read it and paused. The two were quietly talking.

One finally turned, came over to me and with a soft West Indian accent said, "I have to tell you your friend Reenie is dead." I was stunned. I thought back to our days in college, walking in knee-high grass holding hands. The blue sky with white puffy clouds and looking out for the snakes that would slide out of the tall sugar cane seeking sunshine. I remembered sitting on her porch swing at eleven at night drinking iced tea in the tropical heat listening to the tropical birds that would migrate north from Central America. The heat and humidity was so intense we couldn't put our arms around each other without generating more heat.

I met Reenie in August of '73. Her father Tom and my dad were roommates in college in the early forties. In those days, the women stayed in dorms and the men boarded with local houses in town. When my family moved back to the United States from Germany, due to my Dad's fond memories, my parents decided to land in Lafayette, Louisiana. I was enrolled in the university there as was Reenie. Small world. We hit it off instantly.

Our families got together for crabbing and a crawfish boil. She showed me how to catch crab using a chicken neck, a piece of string and a fishing net. Having been raised in Europe I had no idea how this part of America worked. Her family was old landed French and even though she wasn't a Cajun she guided me through the culture of Cajun Louisiana.

In my youth in Europe, the only Americans I met were U.S. Army GIs who had been drafted during the Vietnam War. Their language and slang was colorful. With those experiences implanted, I entered the American dating scene. When I was first dating as a teen in Germany the dating etiquette was a gradual process. The first date was conversation and getting to know each other. The second date, maybe you could hold hands. The third date, if you were lucky enough, a peck on the cheek when you took her home. The fourth date, an actual kiss.

During the crawfish and crab boil, I asked Reenie out. She agreed and we went out on the following Friday night. We went to the off-campus student bars where there was good music, great stories, and a lot of hoots. About midnight I drove her home. Her family home was in the country, a home her father built when he returned from the Second World War. We pulled into the driveway and you could hear the sound of tires crunching the shell paving material. I turned off the car and there was a full moon. I could hear the insects chirping and the parrots from Central America discussing the menu.

"I had a wonderful time."

"Me too."

"My parents aren't home. Would you like to get down?"

I was startled. "Sure."

We went into the house and she made coffee. It was strong and served in demitasses with a plate of small sugar cookies. When I finished the coffee, she politely showed me the door. I got into my car wondering, *What just happened?*

A week later we were on our second date. We were in an off-campus student bar named "The Red Dog Saloon." After a few sips of beer I asked Reenie, "What does 'get down' mean to you?"

She looked puzzled. I reminded her of our last date. She said, "That's an old Cajun expression that goes back to horse and buggy days. When someone came to visit it was polite to ask them into your home. What it means is, would you like to get down from your horse or buggy and come inside?"

I replied, "Let me tell you what it means where I grew up." When I did, she slapped her hand on the bar and exploded. I thought she was going to wet her pants laughing. I loved her dearly.

I laid there staring at the ceiling on the verge of tears.

"What happened?"

"It just says she died of old age."

"How is that possible? She is only fourteen months older than me."

"It is God's Will."

I tried to sit up but my wrists were tethered to the sides of the bed. I stated, "Please untie me, all I want to do is go the chapel and light a candle for her."

"No. That is impossible. You can do it later when you are ready."

"Please. I want to do it now before she gets too far ahead of me." I tried to sit up. She pushed me back down. "Let me go. Let me pray."

She looked down and said, "There will be time for that later."

I started to cry. I don't know if it was caused by the loss of a dear friend or the frustration of my captivity. "All I want to do is light one simple candle for her." I was overcome by many precious memories, much like hearing a long Southern Pacific freight train that would pass through Broussard in the night. The number of cars seemed endless and so were the memories.

The train could be heard every night even though the tracks were miles away. The first time I heard it, I was laying in bed with Reenie. It was two in the morning. I sat straight up and asked, "What the hell is that?"

She rolled over, patted my leg and quietly said, "It's a sound I have been hearing every night of my life." She rolled back over and whispered, "Go back to sleep. It's just a reminder you're alive."

I thought of the next morning when the birds were chirping and eating bananas and bugs, the sun was coming up, shining through the opened screened window. The fan over the bed was clicking like the beats of our hearts. The maid and cook who had worked for the family for years and had raised Reenie and her older sister Mary entered the room.

"Miss Renee, Miss Mary says it's time for you to get moving. Your parents are going to be home soon."

Reenie sat up and announced, "You tell Miss Mary to mind her own damned business."

"Oh no! I am not going to get into the middle of this catfight!" She looked at me and asked, "Mr. Edmund, do you want some breakfast? You got to eat before you go to Mass."

"Yes, please. Two pieces of buttered toast and your wonderful coffee."

"We don't got bread this morning, only croissants."

"Then cut two pieces, toast them the way you always do and serve 'em up with butter and grape jelly. I'll be in the kitchen when I finish shaving. By the way, I'm not Catholic." She deflected that and asked, "What happens if we don't got no grape jelly?"

"We'll just make do with what we have. There's bees out there?"

"Yes, sir."

"Then there's honey."

The memories were so poignant I laid there with tears. The nurse was smiling. "You don't understand. She is not moving away, she is pulling you. She wants you to go with her. And we can tell you she is not afraid., She just wants to walk with you again in the tall grass." I laid there trying to make sense of it. Reenie. Beautiful smile, so full of life. Her snap sense of humor. Her tenderness. I looked up at the nurse and pleaded, "I just want to light a candle for her."

"Sorry. I can't untie you." I was struggling to sit up. They kept pushing me back down. The frustration of helplessness was overwhelming. They left and as I was laying there crying and remembering Reenie, an army medic appeared. He had a cell phone on his belt. I told him what happened with Reenie. If I couldn't light a candle I wanted to send flowers.

He said, "It would be a nice thing to do." He untied my wrists, elevated the back of the bed, handed me his cell phone and said, "I'll be back." He returned with the yellow pages phone book. "Do it quick."

I called a florist and ordered a dozen red roses. I sent them to the last address I knew. The family home outside of Broussard with the crackling shell driveway. The next night, the soldier came back. I used his cell phone to check if the flowers made it. Unconfirmed. I ordered another bunch. The third night, I called to confirm delivery. Unconfirmed. I ordered again for the last time. As I laid there and thought about her I decided I had to escape and go back to that beautiful house and deliver my condolences in person.

I found myself driving through Southwest Louisiana headed toward that old home in Broussard. As I turned onto the crackle of the driveway, I heard the "Caw!" of a crow announcing my arrival. The only person left in her family that lived in the area was her sister Mary. She was a nurse and I didn't know her schedule. I hoped to catch her at home. I pulled up and got out of the car. The tropical heat and humidity dropped on me like a warm wet blanket. I walked up the front steps to knock on the door. I was startled to see three glass vases of dead red roses, wilted from the temperature and dried from the sun. I sat on the porch swing and thought about her. "God bless you, Rennie."

I went back to the car and thought, as long as I have eternity to wander, I should drive over to the Gulf Coast and look at my parents' home. It was on the Gulf Coast of Mississippi. Even though both of my parents were dead, seeing the place where all of us had fond memories would remind me of a more peaceful, carefree time. After that, I would drive to Colorado and try to find Reenie's grave. I also thought that Anne graduated from the University of Colorado, I might find her there, a stretch in logic but I was determined to find her. I wasn't going to quit.

When I arrived at my parents' house, I parked on the street. The house was unoccupied. I walked around to the back yard to see my mother's rose garden. It was overgrown with weeds almost as high as the rose bushes. There was one focal point that immediately captured my attention. In the middle of that weed infested garden there was one perfect pink rose.

Acceleration, ever increasing velocity, deceleration. Thud.

I was sitting at a picnic table in the courtyard of a run-down motel on the Gulf Coast of Mississippi, halfway between Biloxi and Gulfport. I was terribly confused and had no idea how I had arrived there. It was a cheap motel with about fifteen rooms. Looking south, with the sun shimmering off the water, on the left was a diner that was closed. There were vending machines next to the tables. I bought a cup of black coffee. I wished I had a piece of buttered toast to go with it. I was so tired, I remember frequently laying my head in my arms on the table, fighting to breathe. I struggled to understand what was happening.

Suddenly, the thunder of about twelve motorcycles arrived. A crowd of bikers appeared, getting stuff from the vending machines and sitting on the benches of the table. A woman in black leathers jostled my arm and asked, "Do you believe in the death penalty?"

I looked up and replied, "I don't think that is something to believe in but I do support it for those who truly deserve it."

She smiled and said, "Good. We are having a pro-death penalty rally in Colorado in a week. It's at an old Air Force installation where there is space that we have leased. Please show up. I think you might learn something."

"That's pretty arrogant. What is this meeting all about?"

"It's about life. What it means. And the consequences of our choices."

Based on the way they were dressed and their demeanor, I thought these were hardly Ph.D. philosophers. I should have learned in the fifty-two years on this planet that curiosity always causes problems.

"Sounds interesting. Give me the date and time, I'll check it out." I just wanted to breathe normally again. I put my head back into my arms and drifted to sleep.

Acceleration, ever increasing velocity, deceleration. Thud.

As I was approaching the entrance to an unused Air Force facility in Colorado, a remnant of the Cold War, there was Annie Bocquitt sitting on a bench. She was sipping on a tall glass of iced tea. "You don't want to go in there," she said calmly, looking down at her drink, using her right index finger to push a slice of lemon down into the glass.

"Yes, I do. I am curious. Besides, I made them a promise."

"As you will." She smiled, looked up and said, "Keep in mind, more cats have been killed by curiosity than natural causes." I turned and walked to the entrance that had a two-ton blast door that was fully open. "If you do it, it's going to be very hard to get you back and most promises are not well considered."

As soon as I entered the portal, there was an Air Force Captain leaning against the wall. He straightened up when he saw me and said, "Don't go in there."

I continued down the tunnel and was suddenly accosted by four men who dragged me to a room that had a medical examination table in the center. I was forcibly stripped and thrown on the table, my hands tied to the sides and my feet forced into the stirrups and bound. They smeared lubricant on my anus and testicles. Two of them removed their clothes and were in semi-erect state. One had a very large penis, the other much smaller. The smaller one snapped completely erect and went first. I protested and pleaded for him to stop. He smiled and said, "Shut up and learn." He let out a loud groan and pulled out. He stood there for about ten seconds milking his erection, smiled, turned to the other with a much larger member and said, "I have prepared it for you."

The larger one mounted and violently inserted himself. I was pleading for him to stop. I screamed, "God! Please make them stop!" the thrusting continued more violently with ever increasing force and depth. "He . . . stroke . . . can't . . . stroke . . . help . . . stroke . . . you . . . stroke . . . now . . . stroke . . . the . . . stroke . . . only . . . stroke . . . way . . . stroke . . . this . . . . stroke . . . will . . . stroke . . . end . . . stroke . . . is . . . stroke . . . . when . . . stroke . . . you . . . stroke . . . sub . . . stroke . . . mit . . . . stroke . . . to . . . thrust . . . my . . . slam . . . will! Aghaa!" He stayed inside of me for what seemed an eter-nity. I could feel him pulsing and when it subsided, he finally pulled out.

The two were standing between my bound legs fondling each other's testicles. The larger one said, "You have ten minutes to decide. When I come back, it will be with a bigger friend." He grinned, turned around and started to leave. He stopped, turned around, and said, "If you submit, you will be on the other side of this." He smirked and continued, "Apart from certain heterosexual situations, it is better to give than to receive."

"I will not submit."

"Yes, you will." He held up his long fat penis. "He will be ready."

I was trying to focus on the ceiling in a daze. I thought back to my childhood when my brother taught me The Lord's Prayer. I started to recite it: "Our Father, who art in Heaven, hallowed be thy Name . . ."

"I am Captain Roberts." He was whispering urgently. "I work for Colonel Boqcuit. She sent me to get you out of here." As he was talking, he was cutting the restraints from my wrists and ankles. He handed me two wads of toilet paper and continued, "Get dressed fast. You need to get out of here before they realize you are gone." I realized he was the Captain at the entrance. As we were quickly walking out, the Colonel was still sitting on the bench demurely drinking her tea and reading a newspaper. She looked up, smiled and asked, "Did you like that?"

"No."

"Well, here is as little bit of advice; the next time we tell you not to do something and you have a choice, don't do it."

"Where is Anne?" I asked, still stunned.

"Ahead of you."

I went to my rental car and drove back to the hotel. The first thing I did was to take a long hot shower. Sitting in the steam of the shower, I wondered how I was going to find Anne. I remembered she had attended Trinity University in San Antonio, so I thought, *Colorado didn't work.* No listings. Nothing. Even though it would be a long shot, I would go there and try to find her. At that point, I was desperate.

I was on my way to San Antonio but was exhausted and decided to stop for the night in Houston. After checking in, I went to the bar off of the lobby. It was very upscale, predominately black with blue tablecloths and a dark granite bar top. The bar was backlit with deep purple light and there were votive candles on the bar and tables. Slow-moving lasers were casting around and there was soft music that you would find in a nature store. Occasionally, there was a Gregorian Chant.

The bartender in a crisp white shirt and a black bow tie appeared and asked, "What can I get for you, sir?" I asked him for a gin martini straight up with one olive. All I wanted was a stiff cocktail, take a hot shower and go to bed. As I was sitting there, still in a fog and trying to figure out where I was and how I got there I looked over to my left. It was almost a gravitational pull.

There was a man wearing an expensive black suit. We made eye contact. He smiled and asked, "Are you pregnant yet?" I looked at him astonished. I thought he was drunk.

"I have to confess, of all the people I have tried to recruit, you were one of the most entertaining. The pleading gives me a big kick. Most go willingly." I put my drink down and replied, "Get the fuck out before I kill you." He threw his head back, laughed, took a sip of his drink, wiped his mouth with the back of his hand, and replied, "No you won't. That is impossible considering I have been dead for a few thousand years. What makes it fun is keeping up with the latest trends. The old ones— murder, prostitution, homosexuality—they are institutions in any point in history." He smirked and continued. "What amuses me are the new ones like crack and AIDS, Rap and Hip Hop. Even the Heavy Metal shit they call music. 'Highway to Hell.' Those bottom feeders have no idea what they are buying into. I welcome it." With a frightening smile, he continued. "What keeps me entertained is watching how creative humans can be in their continuing methods of descending. It's like fishing. Dangle a good-looking worm and humanity will bite without thinking. The easiest ones to catch are the bottom feeders. The youth with the tattoos and the stolen gold necklaces that think Rap, Hip Hop, and Heavy Metal music will last forever." He smirked. "For them it will. Because they are too dumb to understand; I write the songs. Once I get 'em hooked, they're mine." I looked at him disgusted and remarked: "You are one of the few souls I have ever met that was pure evil. I would rather be bored by Brahms than fucked by Faust."

"That's my point. The vast majority of people choose Faust. In the end, it works out well. I have discovered the source that has allowed me to create an eternal amusement park."

"An amusement park?"

"Not theirs, mine." He paused, lit a cigar, and asked, "Do you remember the coin toss in Kabul? You called my side."

"You were there?"

"You idiot, I am always with you, I am with every man."

"Fuck you. Get away from me."

Acceleration, spinning, ever increasing velocity, deceleration. Thud.

I was waiting in an airport for what seemed to be forever for her flight to be posted as arrived. Even when it was, I knew it would be a longer wait because it always takes longer for people to get off an airplane than to get on. That's why I have always thought when flying: If something happens, everyone is going to die because during an emergency evacuation there will always be some asshole that will try to retrieve his oversized carry-on bag at the expense of every soul on the plane.

When it was apparent she wasn't going to arrive, I went to the airline Help Desk to find out if she made it. The woman working looked as if she either had a long day or a terrible relationship. I said jokingly, "I've lost my wife."

"Is she a bag?"

"Not the last time I saw her. She was pretty good-looking. Could you do me a favor and pull up on your computer and see if she made the flight?"

"No. This counter is for lost luggage. Try upstairs at the check-in counter."

"Thank you. You have been very helpful."

I went up one floor to the check-in area, and there was nobody working the counter, so I sat down in one of three overstuffed chairs surrounding a six-foot by six-foot coffee table. It was soft, comfortable, and conformed to the shape of my body. There were constant announcements for arriving and departing flights. When I heard the announcement for the flight number Anne was supposed to be on, I thought: That flight landed over an hour ago. I tried to get up, but the chair wouldn't let me go. I kept struggling to stand but kept getting pulled back into the seat. I even tried rolling on my side to fall on the floor. It didn't work. There was a man sitting across from me who seemed familiar. He was smiling. He said, "Struggling is pointless."

"Why?"

"Because you are here."

"Where am I?"

"Sitting in a chair that was designed to keep old people from falling out and breaking a bone and then filing for financial compensation from the airport for providing unsafe public furniture." He smirked and glanced at an elderly person sleeping in another chair. "As if she will have some place to spend it. Have you ever used a walker?"

"I'm not sure I understand this conversation. All I want to do is meet my wife and go home."

"That will not happen until she arrives and helps you up."

"Damn this is frustrating. I want to get up!"

"Submit and this will end. Your ten minutes are over." I suddenly recognized him. While his appearance was different, his speech and mannerisms were the same.

"Our Father who Art in Heaven . . ."

"Would you stop reciting that. I don't like that." I looked at the ceiling and asked out loud, "This conversation sounds familiar, how many times do we discuss this? Haven't we had this conversation before? Why should I accommodate you?"

I thought back to my conversation with Ralph on the landing. I smiled and continued. "It's about Will. Mine is greater than yours. Would you rather I tell you to get the fuck out?" I smiled and continued. "In the Bible there is a concept: What the Devil means for destruction, God will turn for good."

I looked over at the elderly lady who was sleeping in the chair next to mine. She was gone. I turned back to the man I was talking with and he was gone. The suction of the chair was also gone. I stood up and walked away, trying to find my wife.

12

Snap, hiss, acceleration, floating in space, deceleration: Thud.

I was sitting at a rest stop in southern Arizona, about five miles from the Mexican border. The stop was a pull-off from the Interstate and had tables and benches. On the table in front of me, there were tiny creatures, about the size of a thumb, dancing all around. I couldn't tell which was the head and which was the tail because they had no face. I remember they were constantly snapping vertically into the air, about eighteen inches high, doing somersaults. I could hear a small snap when they took off.

Struggling to breathe, I watched them for about thirty minutes—until the rodents arrived. They were a bit larger than squirrels, with long brown hair. The most remarkable feature was that they were Cyclopes—one eye in the middle of their forehead. They began feasting on those tiny creatures in a frenzy. I was fascinated that they could catch an object in mid-air without the ability of binocular vision. If you only have one eye, how can you judge distance? One of the Cyclopes had a beautiful coat. The pelt could have been used in any fashion house. He was calmly munching on one of the tiny creatures when a dog—actually, a coyote—exploded from the bushes, grabbed him by the back of the neck, and trotted back into the desert.

All of the other rodents scattered. The tiny creatures stopped popping. I couldn't breathe. I bent over and put my head into my arms. I heard an occasional car blasting down the Interstate.

"*Are you OK?*" The coyote was back. He was sitting across from me licking blood from his paws.

I looked up and asked, "Why did you do that?"

He paused momentarily and replied, "*For the same reason he was eating the Poppers. I was hungry.*" He kept turning his head left to right, looking over his shoulders. He continued, "*What I worry about are the bobcats and lions. They may be hungry as well. A friend of mine, Manuel, was eaten by a lion yesterday.*"

"So, who eats the lions?"

"*I don't know if that's possible.*" He kept looking over his shoulder like a criminal trying to avoid the police. "*There are some animals you can't kill. What makes you feel alive is knowing they are always around you.*" He kept looking over both shoulders, his head turning rhythmically almost as constant as the frequency of a pendulum of a clock. We sat quiet for about thirty seconds and he announced, "*I'm tired. I'm going to sleep.*"

"How can you sleep knowing something wants to eat you?"

He jumped on the ground, looked over his shoulder, and replied, "*You have to find a place you think is safe and leave the rest to fate. The dangerous part is finding your place.*" He turned and trotted off into the brush. I leaned with my head in my arms, trying to breathe, thinking about the coyote. "*Leave the rest to Fate.*" Suddenly, I heard a roar, a high-pitched scream, and commotion in the brush. I looked up, and everything became still. I looked higher and saw the bright stars that can be so beautiful in the night sky of Arizona. He should have said, "Leave the rest to Faith."

Hiss, sizzle, sensation of weightlessness, bang, pop.

Reenie had carved out a chapel in an old salt mine when she was young. She took me there once. It was her private place. It was protected by a lion who lived there. He was a large wildcat native to Louisiana. He would sleep in an altar chiseled into one wall of the room. There was another altar with religious icons.

As I descended into the grotto, I remembered her warning me about the cat. "You can admire him from a distance but if you get too close or try to pet him, he will kill you." During the visit, I was struck by the carved-out altar. There was an old porcelain statue of the Virgin Mary, and many melted and burned-out candles. There were also bones from an animal who died years ago. I looked over, and Reenie was standing there. She was translucent.

I remember that first visit, admiring the animal. "Who feeds him?"

"Coyotes."

"There are coyotes here?"

"They are everywhere. On this level, there are four states of existence. There are poppers, cyclops, coyotes, and lions."

"What about us?"

"We are on a different plane."

I wondered, *Is it possible to juxtapose events from the past to the future?*

Hiss, sizzle, snap, pop, rapid deceleration.

I was sitting at the end of a long mahogany table so highly polished I could see the reflections of paintings on the wall. There was a large crystal chandelier suspended over the middle of the table. I looked to my left and in the adjacent room, there were four men playing cards, drinking from crystal sherry glasses, and smoking cigars. I tried to call out but they couldn't hear me. I tried to stand but couldn't. There was that force again, holding me firmly in the chair. I felt the tightness in my chest returning. I leaned forward and put my head in my arms.

"I have to admit, this has been most entertaining."

My head snapped up and he was sitting at the other end of the table, wearing a blue pin-striped suit, a crisp white shirt, and a burgundy tie, smoothing his Cuban mustache with his right thumb and index finger. Again, he had no reflection. I looked up through the chandelier. I was getting tired of the fight.

"Why me? I've done nothing wrong."

"You dolt! I have selected you not for what you have done. I have selected you for your potential."

"Potential to do what?" I was starting to get visibly angry.

"My bidding. Don't worry, I'll be there to help. I am with you always."

He appeared in the chair closest to my left.

"I told you to get the fuck away from me." I wanted to kill him, but at the same time, I didn't want to touch him. From the far end of the table, he was laughing.

"That is what is going to make it interesting and amusing, watching that Will of yours bend in increments. I can exploit many different situations where you will face a variety of moral choices. The combination of the choices you make will eventually cause you to implode. The stronger your Will, the more entertaining it will be." He stood up, straightened his tie, smoothed his mustache, and slid his chair back. "Well, I will be leaving your consciousness for a while." He smirked and continued, "I have to tend to my roses. I will see you again when you least expect it." I looked for his reflection on the table. Nothing. I looked up and he was gone.

What a feeling . . . dancing on the ceiling . . .

"Stay in the room." Kylie was standing next to the bed. I had just awakened. I hadn't seen Kylie in years. She was standing there with a shaft of morning sun penetrating the windows and dancing on her beautiful blonde hair. She was holding a tray. When Anne was eight months pregnant and we were stationed in Germany, and because the Air Force could send us on a moment's notice to various hot spots South, we decided we needed a nanny. I made the contacts with a few agencies, arranged for interviews, and found Mary Poppins.

"Why?"

With her delightful British accent, she replied, "It could be dangerous until you get used to it. Here is some coffee." The aroma was wonderful, and there were two small sugar cookies on the saucer with a silver spoon.

"Used to what?"

"While you were gone, the laws of physics have fundamentally shifted."

I sat up and took a sip. "Which means?" She gently smiled and put her hand on my forehead.

"There is no up or down. There is no center of gravity. Any surface you choose to stand on seems horizontal. You can walk across a room and encounter a wall. Place your foot on it and keep walking, and when you get to what used to be the ceiling, place your foot on it and keep walking. Every surface you stand on is one 'G'."

"How about the chandeliers and paintings?"

"They stay where they were installed, as you are used to seeing them. When you are standing on a wall, they appear to be suspended sideways. Same as paintings. It's kind of disorienting until you get used to it. I would suggest when you decide to come out, you crawl out on your hands and knees. After a while, the vertigo will leave."

"Is it possible to fall down?"

She smiled and replied, "Yes, we all can, but you have to work at it.

"You are still welcome. Your welcome depends on your choices. Life is good. Enjoy."

Part Three: The Walk Back

Walter Reed Army Medical Center, Washington, D.C. September, 2005

Thud.

My eyes popped open, and I was looking at the suspended ceiling of some room. It was a hospital room in an Intensive Care Unit. I turned my head to the right, and Anne was sitting there. She asked, "Hi. Do you know where you are?"

I looked at her, still thinking I was dreaming. I had to whisper due to the hole in my throat as a result of the surgery and insertion of a respirator tube placed downrange. It had been removed a few days earlier.

"No."

"You are in Walter Reed."

"That's in Washington, isn't it?"

"Yes."

After eight weeks of being dead, struggling to catch up to her, it still seemed to be a continuation of the dream. I reached out my hand. I was not capable of gripping hers. She took mine. I could only whisper, "My God. I have finally found you."

A day or two later, when it was decided I was stable enough to move, I was transferred to what is called the Intensive Care Step Down Unit. The Step Down Unit for my case was an intermediate point from the Intensive Care Unit to the Cardio-

Thoracic Ward. It was also used as an admitting point for Emergency Services. I think they had to park me there until the CT Ward had a room available or staff to deal with me.

I was in a line of ten beds, each of us separated by a curtain that went from the ceiling to about two feet off the floor.

With every new arrival, a doctor would appear and start his memorized speech about "No Heroic Measures." Everyone lying there could hear it. I was heavily sedated and frustrated with my condition. I finally got the attention of a doctor.

I whispered, "Why don't you just tell him he is going to die and get it over with? I am tired of having to lay here all night and listen to you folks break it to them gently. If they want to live, with your help and their determination, chances are they will. In the meantime, I am trying to think. I don't give a shit about their misery. I made it back, and they can too. Instead of reading your 'No Heroic Measures Checklist,' how about telling them they can live if they do what you tell them and believe in something."

He looked at me as if I were crazy.

I continued. "I'll save you a lot of time. Just roll them in here, give me the checklist, and I'll read it to them."

The doctor left, and a nurse who had her family history in the West Indies came to me and started brushing my hair. She said with a delightful Caribbean accent, "We thought you would have learned more than that. Bad news is: You are not back. You are only halfway there."

Early the next morning, I was moved to the CT Ward. Things were looking up. I had my own room, and the staff was wonderful. "Is there anything I can get for you?" the nurse asked. As she was talking, she was writing on a whiteboard next to my bed. She wrote the day of the week, the date, and underneath that information, her name. Her name was First

Lieutenant Laura Criegler. She had the most familiar and pretty smile. There was the delightful fragrance of jasmine in the air.

"Yes. Please, a cup of black coffee and a piece of buttered toast." It had been so long since I had tasted anything.

"We can't do that until you have a swallowing test." She took my hand and continued. "Be patient. You've come this far. You can do this."

I was being fed with a PEG tube into my stomach. The abbreviation is a medical term for Percutaneous Endoscopic Gastrostomy. It is a three-eighth-inch clear plastic tube inserted through the skin and into the stomach, in which the nursing staff would pour enough nutrition into me to keep me alive. It has a small bulb on the end to make sure it doesn't slip back out of the stomach. Over the next few days after insertion, the stomach and exterior skin would close around it. Fortunately, I was unconscious when it was inserted. Unfortunately, I was awake when it was removed. That was also an interesting experience. I had just had the ventilator tube removed from my throat. While there was a valve inserted in the hole, they were worried I would aspirate if I couldn't swallow properly.

"OK, I'll be patient. Changing the subject, there's so much I want to know about what happened when I was gone. For example, did you guys find the animal, or did he just decide to leave?"

"What are you talking about?"

"The animal that was camped out between my calves. He had a habit of kneading my legs with his claws. I thought it was either a large cat or a raccoon. I couldn't understand how someone wouldn't have noticed it. It was furry and quite strong."

She looked at me incredulously and flatly stated, "What you are describing is a Gradient Sequential Compression System for preventing Deep Vein Thrombosis."

"I have no idea what you are talking about but I guess I don't have to worry about fleas, how about the toast?"

"No way."

It was the first week of October, and I felt as if I had been run over by a bus. That was when one of the most negative assholes I ever met walked into the room with a parade of people he was supposed to be teaching about inpatient medicine.

"Allow me to tell you what kind of shape you are in. You have Cryptogenic Organizing Pneumonia."

"What does that mean?"

"Anything about the lung we can't explain. However, due to your lifestyle and chosen location of employment, your lungs have been seriously compromised. Because you have been unconscious for eight weeks, you cannot hold a pencil, stand, much less walk. You are facing at least two surgeries. Expect to be here about six months, after which you will probably be an inpatient in a physical rehabilitation facility for about a year."

I was laying in a hospital bed that was similar to an inflated life raft. At the time, I could not sit up, but I could turn my head. I had been fitted with another, larger valve in my throat so I could talk. I looked over at the doctor, an Army Colonel with a scowl on his face. He had a group of fellows, residents, interns, and students behind him, all Captains in various lengths of white coats, looking at me intently as if I were some kind of specimen. My first thought was, *As hard as I worked to get back, why is he trying to discourage me?* My nurse, First Lieutenant Laura Crigler, stood at the foot of the bed with her familiar smile. I thought, *I haven't been unconscious for eight weeks. I've been dead.* I turned my head, tried to smile, and asked the doctor, "Are you finished?" It didn't sound like my voice.

"Yes."

"Good. Let me explain actually what is going to happen: Two weeks before Thanksgiving"—I held up two fingers and repeated—"Two weeks… I am going home to my family, my books, my cats, and my garden. I don't know what they teach you guys in the Army, but in the Air Force there are two basic concepts deeply imbued in us: The first is, you don't quit. I am going home. I have no intention of spending one night as an inpatient in a physical rehab facility. If I feel exercises are necessary, I will do them at home. The second goal is: Go home. And then, once I feel well enough, I am going to return to Afghanistan and thank everyone still there that had any hand in saving my life. If you don't have anything to contribute to those two goals, I don't need you."

"Are you refusing care?"

"Nope. I am refusing your absence of care."

"You sound angry."

"No. I am looking forward."

All of the doctors and students behind him were staring at the floor. One was a Pulmonary Fellow who I would get to know well through that part of my long walk back. He was assigned to my case. The Colonel didn't want it. He had other patients to discourage. He spun on his heels and marched out of the room. It was as if I had farted in church. All his charges followed without saying a word. Nurse Crigler was still standing at the foot of the bed. She was smiling. The smile was still familiar.

She came around to the left side of the bed and was smoothing out the sheets. As she was working, she said, "I probably shouldn't tell you this, but that doctor is one of the biggest assholes in this hospital. He is a Colonel, I don't think anybody has ever talked to him like that."

"Could be. After all that I have been through, the last thing I need is for some jerk who has never heard a gunshot strut into this room at ten o'clock at night and make a heroic effort to discourage me."

"I think you are going to be well known here."

As she was walking to the door, she turned and asked, "Do you need anything more tonight?"

"No, thank you. And thanks for everything you have done for me. You are an angel."

She smiled and turned to leave and said, "You bet. That's why I wear white. I am charged with helping you go home."

"Hey Lieutenant, what you just witnessed was the beginning of a test of wills which I have every intention of winning." She looked back with that familiar smile and said, "I bet you will."

"Please don't close the door. If you could prop it open with the trash can. I just don't want to be confined anymore." I had never been claustrophobic in my life, but having been restrained during the journey, the ideas of having no freedom had reached the point of being terrifying.

"You got it."

The doctor's orders were to have my vital signs checked every four hours. It was difficult to sleep because a medical technician would crash into the room with a cart, stick a thermometer in my mouth, wrap a blood pressure cuff on my arm, and put a sensor on one of my fingertips. This event happened at ten at night, two in the morning, and again at about six. Compound that with a one o'clock in the morning visit when the janitor would arrive to empty the trash. He would put it back where he was used to seeing it, and the door would slam shut. I would use the call button to the nurses' station and ask if someone would come open the door.

At five-thirty, another crew would arrive with a mobile X-ray machine for a daily chest X-ray. They needed current films for the doctors when they came on shift. It was similar to trying to sleep in the Frankfurt train station. I got to the point where I thought: It would have been easier to just die in Afghanistan. But I always remembered: *"As you will."*

The next morning, after the daily chest X-ray, another doctor arrived. He introduced himself by stating, "I'm Doctor Jordan. I am a psychiatry resident. I thought I would stop by and see how you are doing."

I thought, *Bullshit. I must have really pissed off that Colonel last night.* It hit me that when the doctor got back to his office, the first thing he did was to call the Mental Health professionals. Nobody had ever talked to him like that before.

"I am not exactly in the best of health, otherwise, I am fine."

"What are your goals?"

Just to screw with him, I stated, "To escape."

"Escape from what?"

"Here."

He started down the same road as the doctor the night before. What bad shape I was in, what was in store for me, extended hospitalization, physical rehabilitation, etc. I listened to him drone for about three minutes and finally stopped the monologue. I lifted my right hand, palm forward, and brushed my right ear twice.

There is an interesting aspect about Islam. Whatever language or dialect you use, body language is much more important than in Western civilization. I suppose it has its roots back centuries ago when trading along the Silk Road required personal interaction without the help of translators. The gesture I did would be absolutely understood in the Islamic world: *My ears are full, stop talking, I don't want to hear anymore.*

My wife has always told me I have a tendency to be a condescending asshole. Based on that, I decided to give it my best shot as I was getting tired of these professionals who were supposed to be healing me, not discouraging me. When I used the hand gesture, he stopped in mid-sentence. He was looking at me as if I were going to be a future paper he was going to present.

I smiled at him and said, "I hate to repeat myself, particularly when it comes to matters of importance, but for you, because you seem to be a pretty decent guy, I'll do it one more time." Nurse Crigler was standing at the foot of the bed with her ever-pleasant smile listening to it all. At that point in the exchange, she put her right hand over her mouth.

"Two weeks before Thanksgiving, I am going home. That means if you see my ass dragging this IV pole dressed in these highly coveted Walter Reed pajamas and robe walking down Georgia Avenue, you will know it's two weeks before Thanksgiving. I don't need psychiatric help." I looked at my nurse and continued. "What I do need is a three-hundred-and-sixty-calorie Vanilla Boost because I plan to teach myself how to stand up again, starting today."

"If you try that, you will probably throw up."

"Well, we have both been to college. I suspect it wouldn't be the first time for either of us."

As he was leaving, Lieutenant Crigler returned with a Vanilla Boost. I had to ask her to open it for me because I didn't have the hand strength to do it myself. I knew standing was going to be a challenge. She said, "You need to be careful. You are going to get the reputation of throwing people out of this room who are trying to help you."

I replied, "Oh no. I would never throw anybody out of here who is trying to help me. The only people I'm going to throw out of here are those who want to discourage me or attempt to keep me here longer than necessary. Two weeks before Thanksgiving."

"OK. You know, I'm from Pennsylvania. When I grew up, we always had our Fall festivals." As she was talking, she was folding down the sheet. I now realize she was trying to distract me. I had a catheter inserted in my urinary tract. It was time to have it removed. Lt. Crigler explained the delicacies of removing it. Having never had one installed before, I nodded and said, "Go for it." She pulled back the remainder of the sheet, took my penis in her left hand, grabbed the catheter in her right, and snatched it out. It had been in there for many weeks, and the human body has a tendency to cling on to foreign objects. My eyes were watering. I would have preferred to have been shot.

She looked down at me and asked, "Did that hurt?"

"That was interesting. Do you have any morphine?"

About ten minutes later, the priest arrived. He introduced himself as Father Phillip. I remember thinking, *History doesn't repeat itself, but it does rhyme.* He was a kind man who, as I later found out, visited me every day even when I was not in a conscious state. In fact, when I was in the Intensive Care Unit and most of the staff didn't think I was going to survive, he delivered the Last Rites of Absolution. My wife was sitting by my side and she was too horrified to say anything. Had I been alert, I would have thanked him but explained: I don't need this, I am going home.

Because the army had lost my dog tags at the Aid Station in Kabul, they had me listed as a Catholic. Therefore, I was on the priest's computer printout as a member of his flock. Even in his mid-seventies, he was so full of life and encouragement it was inspiring. When he walked in the room, everything would glow in his presence. The next day he came by to visit on his daily rounds. "I just found out you are not a Catholic."

"That matters?"

"No, but why did you not tell me?"

"For two reasons: First, most of the time I was dead, and second, considering the shape I'm in, I figured I can use all the help I can get."

He laughed and said, "You have all the help you need. Continue to believe in God and yourself, and you will be all right." He turned to leave and paused at the door. "Do you want me to close it or prop it open with a trash can?"

I wondered how he knew that. "Leave it open, please."

He looked at me and smiled and said, "It's your decision."

"Are you coming back?"

"I will always be here." His voice was familiar. Maybe it was from somewhere in the long, continuous dream. I couldn't recall. What I do remember is his presence was a great comfort.

As I was laying there, I was watching CNN reporting on the aftermath of Katrina. I had no idea what had happened. I was dead during the entire event, and my first thought was: *What happened? Did somebody just drop a bomb on that city?* I am sixth-generation New Orleans, the first to leave in decades. Both my mother and father had passed away, so there were not compelling reasons to go back. I have tried to make an annual visit to inspect the family crypt, make sure it was clean, and enjoy the flavor of the French Quarter. After hearing the CNN reporters talking about the looting and the devastation to the Ninth Ward, the incompetence of local and state government, I couldn't help thinking about my father. He once told me: "The people of Louisiana don't want government, they want entertainment." In that same conversation, he explained he would disown me if I ever ran for an elective office in Louisiana.

The news was constantly reporting about the misery of the Ninth Ward. The reporters were droning along about the looting which was taking place. I smirked and thought, *You haven't seen looting until the one hundred billion dollars of federal funds show up.*

I thought about the Ninth Ward. Imagine the worst part of any city in America. Twenty-five years ago, the U.S. Postal Service decided it was too dangerous to deliver mail there. In fact, fire and rescue services would not respond without a police escort. During the rescue efforts, people were standing on the roofs of houses, shooting at the rescue helicopters. The U.S. Government rented over a thousand buses to evacuate the residents of the Ninth Ward and take them to Houston, Little Rock, Memphis, and other cities. The crime rate in all of those destinations shot up. And the entertainment wants it to be a chocolate city again. A large portion of his voter base had left town.

My wife came to visit the next night. She asked me what I thought about Katrina. I told her I had many thoughts about it, but to put it succinctly, I said, "God just flushed one gigantic toilet."

She held my hand and said, "There are many good people down there suffering. I think you are out of your mind."

"Yes, I was for a while, it's called being dead."

"Here are some letters from your sister Betty sent from her school in Denton, Texas." Anne gave me a kiss on the cheek and left. I laid there staring at the ceiling for about thirty minutes and opened the package. I thought about my sisters, Betty, Mary, Melanie, and Laurie. The first letter was a cover letter from Betty, a teacher in a school where the population was predominantly low-income Black and Hispanic. Betty was always upbeat and optimistic. As I read the letter, a flood of memories came back to me.

Betty is only eleven months older than me. I remember once at the dinner table when I was in high school, my parents encouraged us to converse widely on any topic. I announced to the table that I was an accident. My mother almost choked on the dessert, and my stoic father asked, "What makes you think that?"

"Who in their right mind would want to be pregnant for two years?"

My father stood up, placed his napkin on the table, looked at my mother, and said: "I'll be in the study."

I returned to the letter. Apparently, Betty and another teacher who has a brother in the Marine Corps stationed in Iraq organized a letter-writing campaign for me. The entire sixth grade in that school wrote me a letter. It was wonderful to read the thoughts of those kids who were too innocent to understand how the world really works. Betty's cover letter was most interesting, filling me in on all the news of the family.

September 30, 2005

Dear Edmund,

It was a little over five weeks ago when I called your home and spoke with your daughter. Allison informed me that you were very ill. I called because you had promised me you would call at least once every two weeks. I had not heard from you since then, and I was worried about you. Since then, Mary and I have been in touch with Anne. There has been a regular series of phone calls between the three of us. We are thrilled to hear you are improving. Mary and I were quite worried about you. I have so much to say I don't quite know where to begin. So let me start with some questions. . .

What happened? Did you become ill very suddenly, or was it over a period of time? Were you possibly poisoned? Anthrax? You can't imagine some of the scenarios that have gone through my head. *Time* magazine did a big write-up about Afghanistan and what a drug state it is. That even members of Karzai's government are on the take. What do you know?

Mary and Don had quite a time lately. Hurricane Katrina blew out power in DeRidder, and it supposedly will take a week to repair. Mary and Don tried to ride out the storm, but when the power went out, it became oppressively hot and humid. As you know, Don has end-stage diabetes, and the lack of normal environment affected his health, and he began talking and acting strangely. Mary drove him to Patrick's home and later had to hospitalize him. He is now doing better. No damage to their home just as lot of branches down.

Mel, on the other hand, is her usual self-centered self. We did not hear a thing from her for two weeks with no way of contacting her. It turns out that she was safe in Baton Rouge all along with Steve and just didn't feel like talking to us, I guess. Never mind that we were worried about her. She finally contacted Mary. I don't think her home in the Garden District was flooded but probably was looted. We don't know at this point. Mel says that she is going to sell her N.O. home for a million dollars and build one in Baton Rouge. Since the title is in Larry's name, we will see. As a very successful jazz musician, I doubt he will want to leave.

And of course, Laurie is incommunicado. I feel a little guilty when I write that no news is good news here. The last time Laurie called, she ended up staying with us, and it eventually cost us almost $1200 to get her to leave and move back to Louisiana, where of course, she ignored all our advice and began living with the same drug dealers that she was living with before. Even Laurie thinks she is going to have a violent end to her life. How dreadful.

I am sending you some letters from one of the 6th-grade classes at my school. Some of them will crack you up. We are a Title One school, which means most of our kids are poor. Black and Hispanic—but very sweet. Feel free to write back, or not. I hope these cheer you up.

As for me and Danny… Edmund, he is the love of my life. Why I had to wait so long to find him, I don't know. I have to end my letter now, I have another class coming in.

I love you dearly,
Betty

My first thought after reading the letter was: *Thank you, Betty, for that uplifting update.* I can't tell you what I know about Afghanistan. I thought about the poppies in Afghanistan and my sister Laurie. Bottom feeders descend. I decided I was happy to be alive and someplace else.

As I was laying there watching CNN, Wolf Blitzer was hosting his program, which the network decided the theme would be "The End of Days." It was based on the concept that all the natural disasters, tsunamis in the Pacific, hurricanes in the Caribbean, and man-made disasters like AIDS in Africa were somehow related. I don't know whether he wrote that line or some CNN staff intern did, but whoever came up with that premise and wrote that line was an idiot. I remember thinking: It was the most preposterous concept and title ever used. Whoever thought of it hasn't a clue what "The End of Days" means. I thought about William Miller, an 18th-century British theologian who predicted the Apocalypse would happen in 1846. His conclusion was based on mathematical, astronomical, and metaphysical research. I was administered my nightly medications and drifted off to sleep.

Violently decelerate, land, stand in the sand and look over the wall.

The next morning, about an hour after my five-thirty in the morning chest X-ray, I was finally dozing off to sleep when a booming voice came crashing through the door.

"Hi! I'm Doctor McMillian. You probably don't remember me, but I was the guy who did your Open Lung Biopsy when you were in the ICU." He was a huge man. A Major and a Cardio-thoracic Surgeon in the army. He was so large, I don't think Walter Reed had any scrubs that would fit him. Beside him was another physician, Dr. Messinger, an Army Captain who was a CT Fellow. "As a result of the procedure, your left lung has dropped. That's why I want you on this ward. I am going to be managing your case." He turned around and bent over to get a pair of gloves from a drawer, his top part of the scrubs dropped and exposed the top part of the crack of his ass. It reminded me of Dan Aykroyd and Gilda Radner on a *Saturday Night Live* skit. Lieutenant Crigler, who was standing at the foot of the bed, put her right hand over her mouth, made eye contact with me, and we were both silently laughing.

"We could never identify what was the source of the lung infection. We tried every antibiotic we could think of, which would be appropriate but to no result. So my colleagues and I decided on a steroid protocol. It stopped the advance of deterioration, but its effects are going to make it difficult to get that lung to stand up. We are going to have to do another procedure." I asked myself, *How much longer is this going to last?* Another doctor appeared.

"Hi, I'm Doctor Berry, Pulmonary Medicine. Has Dr. McMillian explained what we want to do?"

"Yes, but not the specifics of the operation."

"OK, let me explain. It's not exactly an operation, rather a procedure, but there are certain risks."

The Father arrived. "Another challenge is it?" He arrived after the doctors left. "Well, if you keep believing in two things, you will be alright." I wondered how he knew everything that was going on. He blessed me, and as he was leaving, he turned at the door and said, "Everything will be fine. Do you want the door open?"

"Yes, please."

He winked at me and said, "As you will."

He left, and I picked another letter.

Dear Mr. Mason,

I go to Calhoun Middle School where your sister works. I am in the 6th grade. I hope that you get better soon. I am sorry about what happened. One time I went to the hospital, but it wasn't scary, so don't be scared. Get better!

Sincerely,
Gabriel C.

Two army medics came into the room and transferred me to a gurney on wheels and rolled me to the operating room in the surgical ward. On the way, the hallways alternated between very cold to very hot. As an architect, I thought the building engineer needed to balance the air conditioning system. Thinking back, the temperatures mirrored the swings in thoughts that I was having. The staff was ready, and a female doctor, an anesthesiologist, gave me an exam. I looked up to her and asked, "Before you start, can you give me thirty seconds?"

I woke up in the surgical recovery unit with an extreme burning sensation from my left armpit to my wrist. The nurse gave me an injector to hold in my hand and press a button with my thumb if the pain became too great. I tried it. Whatever the pain killer was, it didn't work. The only comfort was using my right hand to hold my left hand over my right breast. In this position, I felt some foreign objects with my left elbow. There were three tubes coming out of my left side. I called the nurse and told her the injector wasn't doing anything for the pain. She returned and gave me an injection of morphine that helped for about twenty minutes. In this part of the unit, I was one in a line of six beds. I was told I was going to spend the night there. The soldier in the sixth bed on my left had his wife with him. She stayed with him all night, doing the only thing she could do: Be there and encourage him.

"Johnny. Come on, Johnny, don't pull that out. Come on Johnny."

I could tell she was crying. I laid there listening to that chant all night with my arm on fire. Johnny was there, right behind me, slugging it out. Fighting his demons. Refusing to quit. I decided there are three directions of the soul. First, there are souls who don't want to go. What gets them back is sheer force of Will. They are not ready to go and are willing to endure anything to be home.

"Come on, Johnny, hold my hand."

Second, there are souls who want to go. They are souls who had had such a miserable existence, perhaps a horrible cancer or are very old and have no one to return to.

"Hang on, Johnny, don't pull on that. Lie still, please, Johnny."

Third, there are souls who have no choice. Souls who encountered a catastrophic death and going back is impossible. I wondered if he was behind me during my journey or parallel with a vastly different experience. I thought maybe both. "Come on, Johnny, you'll be all right." She was sobbing.

The sun was rising. I looked up to my right, and a nurse was standing there smiling. "How was your night?" The morphine the nurse just administered had kicked in.

"One long, loud groan."

"OK." She smiled and looked puzzled. She patted my leg and told me to use the call button if I needed anything. Five minutes later, there was a commotion down the line. Privacy curtains were completely drawn around us, and everything became deathly quiet.

A few hours later, as I was being moved back to my room on the CT ward, I asked the nurse, "How's Johnny doing?"

"You mean Lieutenant Enswim? He died this morning from head wounds he received in Afghanistan."

"How do you spell the last name?"

"E, N, S, W, I, N. You were there. Did you know him?"

"No. But I know of him." I thought, *He really did exist. I always thought he was one of Stewart's creations. No wonder he wasn't on the Personnel Rolls. He probably worked for Stewart. God Bless him. He fed a lot of children.*

Once I was back on the CT ward, my wife came to visit with my darling daughter. I hadn't seen Allison in months. It was going to be a treat. She was fifteen, and we had many fond memories. I thought back to many times sitting in a café in Italy teaching her shapes and numbers and the alphabet, dancing with her in Budapest on New Year's Eve when she was three, laying on my back holding hands as she jumped on my chest reciting "Hop on, Pop!"

As I was returning from a heavy dose of sedative, I looked over and saw Anne and Allison. Anne kissed me on the cheek. I turned my head to the left and looked at Allison. It was the first time I had seen her since I went to Afghanistan. My blood went cold. As soon as I saw her, I thought, *He's still at it. He's coming through the back door.*

Her once beautiful brown hair was dyed black. There were three studs in each earlobe. She had heavy black mascara, and her fingernails were painted black. As I was looking from top to bottom, I was becoming increasingly more appalled. She was wearing a T-shirt with a heavy metal band logo about death printed on top of a logo of the grim reaper. To complete the outfit, she was wearing a two-and-a-half-inch black leather belt with metal studs and black pants with large zippers on the thighs and calves.

I once again thought, *He's still casting his net, dropping those good-looking worms looking for the bottom feeders.* While I couldn't talk very loud, I exploded. "What the hell is this? You have no idea what you're descending into!" I looked at my wife and demanded, "What have you allowed?" She didn't look like this when I left. Both of you don't understand. He is with all of us constantly.

Anne looked at Allison and said, "He's just coming out of anesthesia." I was finally waking up.

For weeks I laid there with three hoses inserted into my left side, connected to three suction pumps alternating every day from water seal to suction. The only thing I had to do was lay there. I couldn't lay on my left side because I had three hoses sticking out of it. I couldn't lay on my right because there was not enough tube length. All I could do was lay on my back and stare at CNN. I became an expert at analyzing commercials.

"But wait! Order now and you get an additional enema bag for free! Two hundred dollar offer for only nine dollars and ninety-nine cents!" I concluded that pitch meant, Nobody wants to buy this shit and we want to get rid of it.

The second pitch line which I thought was amusing is in every television drug ad: *"Check with your doctor and see if this is right for you!"* It didn't matter if you were suffering from the alphabet of medical problems—Alzheimer's, Beta blockers, Cancer, Diabetes, Erectile Dysfunction, etc. I decided the best thing to do would be when you go to a doctor, rather than recommend a cure you saw on television, explain your problem and let him or her decide what you need. As I was laying there bored out of my mind, I returned to my packet of mail.

Dear Mr. Mason,

I'm a sixth grader at Calhoun Middle School where your sister teaches. Please get well soon. Everybody is writing a letter, and I'm not good at writing (typing) letters, but I'll try. Your family is worried, and I hope you make it. Don't lose hope. You're important to your family. You must be brave. Get well soon, so you can save people. Your job is important. I don't know what else to write.

Sincerely,
Oscar P.

An Army medic pushed a cart through the door. "I got to take your vitals, Sir. Can I have your left arm?" He wrapped a blood pressure cuff on my arm, stuck a thermometer in my mouth, and connected a clip to my left middle finger.

I asked, "Is this really necessary?"

"Doctor's orders. Every four hours."

"Considering I have been dead before, do you think I am going to die again before you come back in the next four hours?"

"Don't know. I'm just following the doctor's orders."

"Are you gonna do this all night?" He was writing his findings in a notepad. "Yep. Like a train. I got to stay on schedule and make sure you're alive."

"What happens if I'm not?"

"Then I won't have to do this every four hours."

When he left, I continued reading my packet of letters from the 6th-grade classrooms.

Dear Mr. Mason,

I am a 6th grader at Calhoun Middle School. I am so sorry that you are ill. I hope you get better soon and figure out what's wrong. But don't give up just yet. Keep your head high and keep doing what you are doing. My uncle is in the military, and his wife and son are so scared as I am. So I hope your wife and daughter are OK. I hope you get better soon.

Sincerely,
Savannah R.

A new young captain arrived. "I'm Dr. Washington… Psychiatric Services." I thought, *How appropriate.*

"I'm doing my rounds and thought I'd stop by to see how you are doing?"

Just to have some fun, I replied, "I'd be doing a lot better if that mirror over the sink would stop staring at me." He looked dumbfounded.

"I understand you were in Afghanistan . . .?"

"I still am."

Laura Crigler started grinning. She knew what I was going to do.

"OK." He paused, studying me intently. "What are you doing there?"

"I am a Fellow in the Afghanistan Mathematical Center for Metaphysical Research and the Director of Logistics for the Afghanistan Right and Righteous Higher Human Transport Company of Kabul."

Laura slapped her hand over her mouth and dashed out of the room.

After he left looking puzzled, Lt. Crigler came back with her ever-present smile. "You do realize when you do that all you are doing is encouraging them to come back."

"Of course. I sometimes need a break from CNN."

The next day, the shrink came back; with him were two senior psychiatrists. One was an Air Force Colonel. He asked me if I knew where I was. I looked at Nurse Crigler. She rolled her eyes, and I replied, "Of course I do. You are where you have been."

The three looked at me intently. Lt. Crigler was smiling. I was getting annoyed with this constant parade of shrinks, so I continued, "You think maybe we could put a 'Group' together so we can discuss where we are? It would be a win-win situation as they say in this town. You could take off half a day, three times a week, and explain to your staff, 'I got Group.' That would allow me to get the hell out of this room and bullshit with people who think they're intellectuals." At that point, Laura lost it. They were all glaring at her. "Hang on a minute… here comes a commercial I haven't seen before. I want to see if something is right for me."

The next morning, I was laying in bed watching the usual cable news blather when Nurse Crigler arrived. "You know that was pretty rude yesterday. I doubt they will come back."

"I know. That was the plan."

"You should apologize."

"Next time they are on the ward, drag them in here and I will. I realize everyone here is trying to help me, but I'm not crazy."

"So how did yesterday help?"

"Less hands, one step closer to being out the door."

"Interesting you should bring that up. We have decided you are going to walk." She stated it as if it was given. The priest was standing behind her.

The Father said, "You can do this. You've fought hard to get here. Remember the two things."

I looked at them as if they were crazy. I couldn't sit up.

"Give me your hand. It starts with sitting up."

Nurse Crigler was direct. I held my left hand out, she gripped it, and pulled me to a sitting position. "Practice that, and when you get the hang of it, then try turning sideways and flopping your legs over the side of the bed. Keep your call button in your hand in case you fall out." I laid back and thought, *This isn't going to be easy. It's going to be pure Will.*

I picked up the pack of letters from the table next to my bed.

Dear Mr. Mason,

My name is Gwi. I am very glad that you are helping those people. I wonder what had caused your sickness. I think it was the heat or water. How many years do you think it will take to rebuild everything? Well, it was nice writing to you. Thank you.

Sincerely,
Gwi

Rebuild everything? Is she asking about Afghanistan or me? We are both in the same condition. As I was laying there unable to walk, I was thinking what I was going to design for my house in the event I had to go home in a wheelchair. I pushed those negative thoughts behind me and picked up the next letter. It was the right message at the right time.

Dear Mr. Mason,

I'm a sixth grader at Calhoun Middle School where your sister teaches. I hope you get better soon so you can go see your family. If I was in your position, I'd be wondering how I got sick in the safe house and also be thinking if I'm going to survive or not. I'd also be thinking, if I survive, then how would I have to live? Well, I hope you survive.

Sincerely,
Irene N.

In the continuing hours and days, I practiced sitting up. When I finally got the hang of it, I decided to try flopping my legs over the side of the bed. I got pretty good at it. A few days later, a lovely nurse who took care of me at the beginning of my stay at Walter Reed came into the room. I couldn't remember her name, but I remember her constant optimism. She saw me sitting on the side of the bed and stopped in her tracks. Her smile was electric.

She walked over, stood between my legs, put her hands under my armpits, and said, "Let's see if you can stand on your own." She lifted me off the bed. My feet hit the floor, and I had to hug her to keep from falling. She laughed and said, "Look at you! You're standing!"

She was as tall as me, and I could feel her breasts pressed against my chest. I remember the embrace was so wonderful I smiled and asked, "Do you want to go dancing when you get off?"

"Dance the night away..."

After much practice, I discovered over time that if I sat up, flipped my legs over the side of the bed, placed my palms on the side, and slid off, I could stand on my own. I would do that twice a day, and as I was standing, practice doing toe-stands, ten at a time for about thirty minutes. I got pretty good at it. The hard part was climbing back into the bed. The effort was similar to climbing into a life raft in the ocean.

Learning how to walk again was one of the most challenging parts on the journey. It was similar to watching a toddler take two uneasy steps and fall on their butt. Because I had three tubes sticking out of my left side connected to suction pumps alternating from "suction" to what was called "water seal," I had to arrange in advance when I wanted to try walking. The army medics would come into my room, disconnect the hoses from the permanent machine, and reconnect them to portable machines and strap the devices onto an IV pole with wheels. The first time I tried it, I used a walker you normally see in a nursing home. I needed it for support and balance. The nurse was at my side, pulling the IV pole, and an army medic was behind me, pushing a wheelchair in the event that I ran out of gas.

On the first attempt to walk, I made it about one hundred feet from my room. I managed to get to the elevators when I had to sit down. As we were rolling back, I looked at my nurse's smiling face and said, "The upside to this adventure is, if this place ever catches on fire, I can get out of here on my own."

She smiled and said, "You shouldn't use an elevator during a fire."

"I know. But the stairs are right next to them."

"The Physical Therapist hasn't started you working on stairs."

"I know. I would slide down on my butt if I had to."

As I was being rolled back to my room with an army medic pulling the IV pole behind me, Nurse Crigler resumed the conversation.

She smirked and flatly stated, "You sound as if you have it all figured out."

"No. I don't have it all figured out. I just know I am going to survive this. I am looking forward."

As we were rolling, she bent down, gently caressed my chin with her right hand. There was a scent of jasmine. She gave me that familiar smile and said, "I bet you will."

I decided those elevators were going to be my benchmarks for progress. I was flying a mile ahead of myself. "If anything ever happens, focus your efforts on people who need help. In an emergency, don't worry about me. I will survive."

When I got back to my room and flopped in bed, I returned to my letters.

Dear Mr. Mason,

I am a sixth grader, and I just want to tell you that I believe in you. Ms. Storrie told us a lot about back ground, and you sound like a pretty good guy. And I would also want to tell you that we have you all in our heart, and God loves you. I would hope to see you soon.

Sincerely,
Carion L.
P.S., God bless you.

The next day, I made it past the elevators. The design of the hospital was similar to city blocks. I decided I was going to walk around the block. With my enthusiasm, I set too fast a pace and realized I was having a hard time breathing and was leaning on the walker. I refused to sit in that wheelchair behind me and finally made it around the block and back to my room. I climbed in bed and asked the nurse for some oxygen. As I laid there breathing deeply, a commercial for the "Scooter Store" came on. I was determined I wasn't going to accept that. I had that will to walk and decided I was going to walk two weeks before Thanksgiving. Laying there with a clear plastic tube that had two outlets stuck in each nostril, there was a lingering thought that I wasn't going to make it back to how it used to be. Then I would think about that asshole doctor and remind myself, two weeks. "My will is greater than yours." You don't quit. I read another letter from the school.

Dear Mr. Mason,

I am a 6th grader at Calhoun Middle School where your sister teaches. See, my sport is football, and my only fear is that I will break my leg for good. I wish that they would fix you up. Everyone here hopes you get better soon, even your family does too. See, my life is hard cause school, but I get my work done to be good. A promise is a promise, you got to get your work done.

Sincerely,
Anthony P.

Staring at the ceiling, I thought, *Two weeks before Thanksgiving*. After reading that, I decided it was time to make a schedule to practice walking. I just hoped I wouldn't break a leg for good. A promise is a promise.

"Hi. You're still here." The young psychiatrist popped in the room. I admired his persistence.

"No, I'm not, and neither are you."

"Interesting. My approach, my counseling technique is using logic."

"That's a slippery slope to go down. For example, using logic, I can prove you are not here."

"Try."

"OK. There is an ancient Greek approach to find the truth just by asking questions."

"I know who you are referring to."

Laura rolled her eyes and said, "Hold that thought. I got to get a witness." She went into the hallway and grabbed the first person available. He was Dr. Berry, who had assisted in my surgeries. He was a Pulmonary Fellow who had known the other docs in psychiatry a long time. He had a grin on his face. The nurse told him that I was going to prove the psychiatrist wasn't there. He seemed to have a friendly professional difference with the shrink.

I continued my thoughts. "Are you in London?"

"No."

"Are you in Rome?"

"No."

"Are you in Paris?"

"No."

"Well, if you aren't in any of those places, that means you have to be somewhere else, right?"

"Right."

"And if you are somewhere else, you can't be here."

The pulmonary doc laughed out loud and walked out of the room.

The Captain popped in a big grin and stated, "I'm going to write down you are full of shit and certifiably sane."

"If I told you that in the beginning, would you have believed me?"

"No, but just for the entertainment value, I'll be back."

"Please do. It would be a nice break from CNN . . . Look! Another Right for You ad. It's a new one. My favorites are also the Scooter Round electric chairs. You look at the folks riding them that are so damned fat, if they got out of the chair and started walking, they wouldn't need them." Looking back, I think a part of Ralph rubbed off on me.

The next day, I was laying there watching CNN, and the whole "Scooter" Libby issue developed. I was amused. Dr. Berry came in the room, saw me watching CNN, and asked me, "You have been over there, what's your take on this?" I wonder if he really knew what I was doing in that part of the world.

"Been doing a lot of musing. You got any cigars?"

"No."

"What kind of covert CIA officer on a daily basis walks through the front door of CIA Headquarters? She is about as covert as Bob's Big Boy. What kind of secret identity do you have when you allow yourself to be photographed in a red sports car and have your smiling face plastered on the cover of a national magazine? She wasn't a Case Officer, and she and her husband are political animals sucking on one of the tits of Washington. Too bad the press buys into this bullshit and feeds it to the American public." I was thinking about guys like Stewart, pounding the dirt streets of Afghanistan wearing a burka and a gun, risking his life and avoiding publicity to do his job.

"The big story should be: If a blonde Caucasian female can work covertly as a Case Officer in the Middle East, or Central and South America, or Asia, without attracting attention, it would be an astonishing feat. And now, a faction in this city are going to ruin a man's career because they don't like his stupid nickname and who he works for." I had a flight of ideas.

"When I was a young boy, all of my sisters called me 'Bubba.' On my sixth birthday, my mother announced at dinner to my four sisters that I was going to be called 'Edmund,' and I was no longer going to wear short pants. I thought, if you keep a childhood nickname like 'Scooter' and want to deal at that level, you are inviting scrutiny. At the same time, I couldn't help but think, *This whole issue is organized by leftists who are pissed off that Bush got elected twice.* When Clinton was in office, they were making great strides in implementing their agenda. Blow jobs were no longer sex, it's just heavy petting. Daily business in the White House was a constant pizza party in jeans. Jimmy Buffet once wrote a song titled 'Gypsies in the Palace.' So getting back to your original question. She sends her husband to Africa to meet with a dictator who is basically a caveman and doesn't know shit about nuclear physics and they sit around drinking tea and he is reassured there was no transfer of that kind of material or technology to Iraq. The whole pile of crap about no weapons of mass destruction in Iraq before the invasion is just that: A pile of crap. Of course there were. The problem is they can't be found because they're somewhere else."

"Interesting observations. Got any discomfort?"

"Yeah. From all directions."

"Hi. I am Doctor Messinger, Doctor McMillian's slave. I will be taking over your case for a while." Lieutenant Crigler was standing at the foot of the bed. She turned to the sink and started to wash her hands.

"Where is Doctor McMillian?"

"He is at a scientific conference in San Antonio eating Mexican food and thinking about you."

"Well, he is a caring person. I'm sure I will be on his mind when he is sitting on the River Walk, drinking a Margarita, and dipping his tortilla chips into the guacamole."

"I just found out you are an Episcopal." He squinted with a smile. "I know all about you guys. I went to an Episcopal Junior High School and a Jesuit High School. What I discovered was the Episcopal Church is all the pageantry and half the guilt."

I had never heard religion compared to a light beer before, but he had a point. "When you get there, take it up with Henry the Eighth, if you can find him."

Suddenly, Ralph came blasting through the door. He was dressed in seventies blue plaid pants, a white sateen shirt with a green tie that had the logo of some Irish family. The best accent was the red and white size nine bowling shoes which he probably swiped from a bowling alley the day before. I knew they were size nine from the white leather numbers stitched on the heels.

"I heard you were sick, so I thought since I was in this neck of the woods, I would pay you a visit. Damn, you look like shit."

"Thank you for your observation, Ralph. It's a good thing you didn't go into medicine." Dr. Messinger was trying to do everything he could to keep from laughing. He turned his back to us, put his hand on the wall, and was silently laughing.

"So, what are you doing back here?"

"Working as a Budget Analyst for the fucking Peace Corps."

"Well, it's good you are in a position where you don't have to carry a gun."

"Of course I do. This is Washington, D.C. It's in the car. I didn't think it would be polite to bring it into a hospital." At that point in the conversation, I thought Dr. Messinger was going to wet his pants. Nurse Crigler put her right hand over her mouth.

Just then, a young captain, a physical therapist, walked in the room with a bunch of twenty-four-inch, one-inch-wide rubber bands. I had met with her earlier that day. She explained they were good for working out while lying in bed. The idea was to tie them to the rails on the bed and to use them to work out for resistance exercises. Ralph was studying them intently. He finally asked, "You got any more of those things? They would be great to snap people on the butt. It would be my way of reaching outside the box."

The captain looked at Ralph amazed and asked, "Are you a psych patient? Which ward are you on?"

"The fucking Peace Corps."

Again, Nurse Crigler put her right hand over her mouth. Dr. Messinger, leaning on the wall, finally started laughing out loud. He looked at me and I said, "I'm not a physician, but I made the diagnosis a long time ago."

"Hey, I got to go back to work. I'm working on a plan to extort as much money as we can from the American people. The idea is: The more money we can get, the more time we have to travel the world, sit around and self-actualize. Hand out a few condoms, tell people we are making an effort, well up emotion and explain what we are doing is important." He smirked at me and continued. "It's in perfect keeping with John F. Kennedy's lifestyle and vision. Camelot was a bunch of bullshit. I'll stop by again. Hope the next time I see you, you don't look like shit."

He pulled out a pack of Lucky Strike cigarettes, took one out of the pack and started to light it. Lieutenant Crigler shouted, "Don't light that! There is oxygen in here!"

Ralph said, "You're right. The man has been blown up once. Twice would probably kill him."

"Thanks for coming, Ralph." He left, and I thought his whole life was filled with luck. Eventually, explosive gases combined with Lucky Strikes would be his demise.

"Good morning. I'm Captain Culpepper, the Duty Chaplain."

He looked like the guy who used to run ten miles a day around our office in Kabul. The guy we called the "second hand." He seemed to be a young enthusiastic minister determined to save souls. I looked over and noticed the cross above the left breast pocket on his uniform. "What denomination are you?"

"Evangelical. I am making my rounds and was told you could use some spiritual counseling. We are all sinners. The best way to repent is to explore the questions that confuse our lives and to admit our mistakes. There are many questions about life and many mistakes we have made. What are yours?" I had no intention of telling someone I had never met before about those details of my life. Those psychiatrists put him up to this.

"What you are talking about is imploding."

"I don't understand."

"I do."

To make it fun, I continued. "As a member of the Coptic Church, do you know John the Baptist is buried in Egypt without his right arm from the elbow down? The remains reside in a golden box in the hall of treasures in Topkapi Palace, the seat of the Ottoman Empire in Istanbul."

"No. I didn't know that. How do you? By the way, I'm not a member of the Coptic Church."

"How does anybody know anything for certain? Without proof, all you have is to believe it to be true. I've seen the arm but not the body. Besides, a merchant in a bazaar in Istanbul was trying to sell me an inkwell assured me he was buried in Egypt. This could lead to a much longer conversation. The purpose of dismemberment in Islamic culture, for example. Back to your original questions, I only have one question about my life." I started twirling a pencil through the fingers of my right hand and asked the ceiling, "It is: Why is it every time I am sitting on the toilet smoking a cigarette, that's the only time anyone calls me on the phone? The biggest mistake I have ever made is not to have had a phone installed on the wall right next to the toilet." His jaw dropped. Nurse Crigler put her hand over her mouth and dashed out of the room laughing.

I was discharged two weeks before Thanksgiving. I remember standing in my room, clean hair, freshly shaven, and dressed in normal clothes, staring out of the window. It was gray and raining, and I thought of Islamic teachings: *Angels come down with every drop of rain.* I marveled at the remarkable life's experience I had endured. All I had to do at that point was to get the discharge papers and have them coordinated with the pulmonary medicine doctor. Anne arrived to help me gather my things and drive me home.

Dr. Messinger came in the room with the necessary paperwork and prescriptions. Because I was being discharged with three tubes sticking out of the left side of my torso, four inches in length connected to three small plastic containers, he explained the prescribed medicines and the schedule for having the tubes removed. When he was finished, we shook hands, and I thanked him for everything he had done for me. As I was leaving, I asked him if he knew where Laura Crigler was. I wanted to thank her as well. I was going to miss her familiar smile and the fragrance of jasmine.

"Don't know. She was reassigned yesterday."

"Any idea which service?"

"No. This hospital is too big."

Staring at the rain, I thought back to somewhere in my past. I read: *"Angels are a signpost of the presence of God."*

Anne and I slowly walked out of the ward as she gently held my elbow because my balance wasn't normal. We walked to the Pulmonary Services area and met with Dr. Berry. He did a brief exam and signed the required paperwork. Smiling broadly, he said, "Follow me. There is someone I want you to meet." We walked down the hall, turned a corner, and stopped at an office with an open door.

The sign on the door stated: Pulmonary Program Director.

Dr. Berry knocked on the door, smiled, and said, "Colonel, it's two weeks before Thanksgiving."

Leaving the hospital, my wife, still holding my elbow, sat me on a bench outside the main entrance and said, "Wait here, I'll get the car." She left, and about ten seconds later, I was surprised to see Dr. Annie Bocquiat appear. She gave me a big hug and a smile and asked, "How are you feeling?"

"Getting better every day. What are you doing here?"

"I'm in town for a conference, and I decided to stop by and see old friends. I stopped by to see you, but I was told you had already left."

Anne pulled up in the car and got out to help me. She asked, "Why are you talking to yourself?" I looked over and Dr. Bocquiat was gone.

"I'm talking to the raindrops."

"Do you want to go back inside?"

"No. I want to go home."

In January, I had a follow-up appointment with Dr. Berry. He met me in the waiting room and escorted me to his office. I took off my shirt, and while he was examining me, he said, "I did a lot of research about your condition. Your case is being presented to scientific conferences all over the country."

"Why?"

"Well, I did some research and found there have been fourteen cases like yours who returned from Afghanistan and Iraq. Twelve were dead within thirty days. We have one who arrived a week ago, and he is in the ICU. You're still standing."

"I hope he makes it. Tell him it's all a matter of a combination of your skills and his will. He may seem to be out of it, but he can hear you." *Come on, buddy, we won't quit if you don't quit.*

After I left his office, I decided to drop by the CT ward and say hello to the folks that were so kind to me. I was walking down the long halls of the hospital where I worked so hard relearning how to walk. I turned a corner near the Intensive Care Unit and encountered two nurses in hospital scrubs.

"My God! You are alive!" one of the nurses exclaimed.

"Yes, I am."

I looked at the two nurses who appeared to be exhausted and wondered who they were. "I'm sorry, but I don't know who you ladies are."

They both blossomed with huge smiles. The nurse on the right said, "We took care of you in the Intensive Care Unit. None of us thought you were going to make it. It's so wonderful to see you standing up and walking. I never would have guessed you are as tall as you are."

The nurse on the left said, "Welcome back… may I ask you a personal question?"

"Sure, after what I have been through, modesty is gone."

"What is it about roses?"

The question startled me. I was thinking, *She couldn't know that… My father said when I was young, about my mother's roses, the roses in Italy, the roses in Arizona, the roses in Maryland, or the roses of Kabul.*

"What are you talking about?"

"When you were in the ICU and things looked grave, the priest administered your Last Rites, your wife was sitting at your side. We knew she was an Episcopalian. She was looking at the monitors and could tell what was happening. A couple of times, she gently shook your arm and said, "Come on, Ed, it's time to be a rose.""

I thought of the train station in Ljubljana. I remembered Anne on the platform holding my daughter and shouted as the train was departing, "I'll call you when I think you are home!"

"It's about a seed planted many years ago."

I walked out of the hospital and into the parking garage and made the long drive home. It gave me time to think about what had happened over the past year. After pulling into my driveway, I walked to the backyard and, leaning on a cane in my left hand, surveyed my rose garden. My thoughts went back to my mother, her roses, and a conversation we had when I was in college. I had overslept and was in my parent's kitchen pouring coffee. I was going to be late for class. She walked in and, frustrated with what she perceived to be my lack of focus asked with her soft Southern accent: "Edmund, what are you going to do with your life?

"I don't know, but it's going to be interesting."

I looked at the task at hand, what I had to do to put the rose garden in proper order. There was a broken flower pot Anne bought in Mexico. It must have blown off the deck while I was gone and landed on the stones I had placed to surround the garden. I remember looking at the shards and thinking what Ernest Hemingway observed: "Life changes us all, but some of us emerge as more than broken pieces."

As I was looking at the roses, I noticed: Even though it was January, there were the remains of one in full white bloom. I thought of the concept I read many years ago, about the "Primacy of Divine Grace over all Human Efforts." You are where you have been. I touched the rose, watching my frozen breath in the cold winter air, put my hand over my heart, and silently said, "Thank you."

My cell phone rang.

"Hi, Ed. Jack Grot. Glad to hear you are out of the hospital. You feeling OK?"

"Getting better every day."

"Good. I got a job for you. Do you want to go to Baghdad?"

"Hell, no."

About the Author

Edmund B. Mason earned his B.F.A. degree at the University of Louisiana and his master's degree from Central Michigan University. He served in the United States Air Force as a Logistics and Engineering officer and worked for many years in Turkey, North Africa and Italy. After his Air Force career, he worked for a defense contractor. Following his illness, he retired and tended to his rose garden and wrote from his home in Maryland. Mr. Mason passed away in 2011.

This is his first published book.